LISETTE DAVENPORT

Whispers of Christmas
A Whispers Novella

First edition

ISBN: 978-0-6459323-2-4

This book was professionally typeset on Reedsy.
Find out more at reedsy.com

For my mother, who introduced me to the genre.

Acknowledgement

Thank you to Claire Selishta at Quill and Scroll Proofreading and Editing for her support. http://quillandscrollproofreading.co.uk

One

Chapter 1

Lady Daphne Brookshire despised Christmas. She scowled as a parade of servants hauled box after box of glittering Christmas baubles into the grand foyer of Brookshire Manor. Pine garlands and ribbons of red and green emerged, soon followed by enormous bundles of holly, ivy and mistletoe for the great hall. The smell from the mixed woods permeated the air, making Daphne feel nauseous.

'Must we endure this tedious spectacle again?' Daphne clenched her fist, nails digging into her palm.

'But my lady, Christmas is a time for joyful traditions!' her lady's maid, Helena, replied. Rosy cheeks beaming, she held up a golden wreath dotted with candles and delicately painted glass ornaments. 'This one is my favourite.' Several maids came giggling through the open front door, followed by two grooms hauling a large crate of Christmas decorations between them. A cold wind sent flurries of snowflakes onto the tiled floor.

Daphne rolled her eyes at the bright-eyed maid. 'Balderdash.' The scene before her brought back reminders of a past that ruined Christmas. She wanted no part of such cloying rituals, not after the awful Christmas two years prior. Lord Alfreton had so callously broken her heart right before the holiday season, leaving her whole world shattered, she had been so crestfallen

1

and unable to eat or sleep. The sound of the parlour pianoforte playing festive tunes made her visibly wince. Garlands of holly pricked her fingers, mistletoe mocked her heartbreak. This year, the familiar comforts of home felt suffocating, reminding her of all she had lost.

Now the mere thought of mandatory social gatherings, gifts, feasting, and jovial carols repulsed her. The London elite had even branded her 'Miser' last year when she had outwardly scowled at platters of shortbread shaped like wreaths and scoffed at bouquets of mistletoe. She had fled to the country this year, but still, the spectres of Christmas haunted her even here.

Daphne's youngest sister, Sophie, came bounding down the stairs; her face full of joy at the masses of decorations the servants were erecting in the great hall. 'Daphne, can you believe Christmastide is almost here? Aren't the decorations marvellous?'

'Downright gaudy, if you ask me.' Daphne picked through a box of silver candle holders, embroidered stockings, and brightly painted nutcrackers. 'I'm sure all this pomp and circumstance will not last. Give it a few years and I'm sure it will be back to the old, special mass and extra special dinner.'

'You truly are turning into an old miser sister! I do hope you'll be on your best behaviour tonight at the Wintershire's holiday ball.'

Daphne grimaced, having forgotten that the first torturous Christmastide event of the season was upon her. She contemplated feigning illness to avoid the cacophony of cloying carols and suffocating scents of cinnamon and nutmeg that were sure to pervade the gathering. But she knew their mother would never allow such truancy from her duties.

'Very well, I shall make an appearance, but I refuse to don some gauche red gown simply because it is Christmastime,' Daphne declared. 'In fact, I shall wear my black silk to deliberately drain the holiday spirit from that garish gathering. If you will excuse me, I have some glowering to do in my rooms'.

As Daphne swept from the room, Sophie and Helena exchanged worried glances. The surrounding air seemed to crackle with the strain of Daphne's anger, and they looked at each other uneasily. 'I do wish we could restore her Christmas cheer,' Sophie said sadly. Helena shook her head after her mistress and continued to carry garlands and wreaths into the main hall. The scent of fresh flowers swirled in the breeze she created, filling the room with a rich sweetness.

* * *

As Sophie fluttered about decorating the halls with wreaths of holly and boughs of fir, her enthusiasm was tempered by frustration. The heavy garland kept drooping under the weight of the silver candle holders and embroidered stockings.

'Oh fiddlesticks!' Sophie huffed as she stood on her tiptoes to re-position the garland for the third time. 'This simply will not do.'

The maids exchanged amused glances as Sophie scowled in a manner reminiscent of her older sister. Though sweet-natured, Sophie's impatience sometimes got the better of her. 'Let me help, my lady,' said one of the maids, taking pity on Sophie's struggle. Together they managed to securely re-hang the garland.

With the decor back in order, Sophie's irritation vanished instantly. She resumed humming snippets of carols while dotting the garlands with cranberries as red as her wind-chapped cheeks.

Through the open doorway Sophie saw a young footman, no more than eighteen, descend from his horse. He swung his leg over the saddle and dismounting, almost tripping as he did so. Exchanging a few words and passing a note to the head butler, he hopped back on his stead and rode off. Curious, Sophie stepped outside into the front entry, where the butler was pulling the doors shut behind him. 'Thomas, who was that young man sent from?'

'The Duke of Hazelbury, my lady. Seems the duke has taken up residence at Jasper Park for Christmas. He wishes your father to call on him during the week.' Thomas strode towards Lord Brookshire's study. Sophie wrinkled her nose; she wanted nothing to do with Hazelbury. His grandson Edward had been a childhood friend of her brother, James'. He had roped Daphne and her into countless games with James and their cousin, but he had moved to the continent several years ago and was unlikely to return until he had made his own fortune. However, this bit of gossip must be shared, and she took off in search of her mother.

* * *

Daphne watched the footman ride away from her bedroom window. She hoped it was not another invite to some horrible Christmas event. The drapes shuddered slightly in the wind from the open window, as she shuffled through her stack of cards, looking for the ones that she knew she had to attend and the ones she could toss into the fireplace. Vacant slots on her calendar opened up with every note she burned, and Daphne revelled in the thought of being able to have a nice quiet dinner among family.

* * *

'Mother, I have something to tell you,' Sophie said, taking a seat beside Lady Jane. 'It seems the Duke of Hazelbury has taken up residence at Jasper Park for Christmas.' She relayed the rest of the details with growing excitement.

Lady Jane smiled benevolently. 'How lovely. It will be good for your father to reconnect with the Hazelbury family.'

Sophie shifted in her seat. 'Well, I thought it was interesting news…' She looked down, trying not to feel hurt by her mother's lukewarm reaction. Sometimes she still felt like a child vying for attention.

Lady Jane, noticing Sophie's change in demeanour, put her embroidery down and reached out and patted her hand. 'Forgive me, dear. You're right, this is noteworthy information. You have such a talent for gathering the latest gossip.'

Sophie brightened at the praise. She resolved to pay more attention to society's happenings from now on. Perhaps she needn't always stand in her sister's shadow after all. Sophie swished her skirts as she left the room, mentally checking off all the acquaintances she had to catch up with at the ball that evening.

Later that afternoon Sophie sat with her mother in the drawing room drinking tea. 'Your father informed me that the Hazelbury dukedom has changed hands. The old duke passed away last week. The new one arrived from the continent yesterday.' Lady Jane Brookshire peered over her teacup. 'Edward has supposedly brought a friend back from the continent with him. Your father and James will be going to see him the day after tomorrow. Hopefully, they can organise for you and Daphne to have an invitation.'

'Mamma!' Sophie placed her teacup back on the saucer. 'You have no idea if the new *Duke Hazelbury* or his friend are looking for wives. And it is not like we need an invitation to see Edward. We practically adopted him as a child like a lost puppy. No, Edward is family, so I do not know why we would need an invitation. Admittedly I have not had a letter from him in some time. Let the poor men at least get the lay of the land before you start foisting every eligible young lady on them. Your matchmaking interference can be a bit much sometimes.'

'Nonsense!' Lady Jane waved her hand in dismissal. 'The incident with Lord Henry was an accident, how was I to know the poor girl had bad vision. Her mother, very rightly, had kept that a secret. And I did help Lady St. Claire set her daughter up with Lord Avery, it is not my fault the silly girl broke it off and chose Mordesley, though he was the better match indeed. Anyway, I was not wanting to match them up with anyone, just you girls.'

'Mother! You know Daphne would kill you if she heard you speak so. Alfreton really upset her. Oh!' Sophie put a hand to her mouth. 'You do not think Alfreton would dare be at his country home for Christmas with his wife? They stayed away last Christmas but with their estate not 10 miles away, they may wish to frequent some of the same balls. Oh, Daphne would be mortified! We do need to find something that would give her some cheer at this time of year.'

'I have not heard the whereabouts of Alfreton, though they may retire to the country with their new child. Brace yourself for the Daphne storm, should they grace us with their presence.'

* * *

That night, Daphne descended the grand staircase at the Wintershire's country manor her dark attire drew the eyes of the assembled partygoers. She strode past the massive display bedecked in candles that filled the hall with a warm glowing light. She didn't indulge in a single piece of shortbread or cup of wassail, instead brooding in a shadowy corner as the London elite danced joyfully amidst garlands of evergreen boughs and ribbons.

'Really, must there be mistletoe everywhere? How unseemly,' Daphne declared loudly to her friend Lady Emma.

'Don't be such a miser, Daphne! Mistletoe and holiday cheer are tradition!' Emma replied with a laugh.

Daphne's mood only darkened with each successive carol, and she vowed to herself that this year, she would be the most wretched holiday miser that England had ever seen.

The Christmas music faded as Daphne's thoughts drifted back to that disastrous holiday season two years prior. She had been so blissfully in love with Lord Henry Alfreton and thought he felt the same.

Arm in arm, Daphne had strolled with Lord Alfreton through the bustling Christmas market, her cheeks rosy from the bracing winter air. As they passed stalls selling roasted chestnuts, spiced cider, and glittering ornaments, Lord Alfreton gazed at her as if she was the only person in the world.

"My beautiful Daphne," he murmured, bringing her hand to his lips. "Allow me to select the finest of these flowers for you."

Daphne's heart had thrilled as he chose an enormous bouquet of holly, pine, and mistletoe tied with red velvet - the largest arrangement at the stand. Its scent enveloped her, conjuring visions of a future filled with joy.

That night at the candlelit Ball, Lord Alfreton had whirled Daphne around the dance floor until she was breathless. As the string quartet played a soulful cello solo, he drew her close and whispered "You are exquisite. Being with you feels like magic."

Daphne had gazed into his smouldering eyes, certain that this must be true love. The cellist's dolce tones swelled around them as Lord Alfreton pulled her into an alcove, hidden by garlands. When Lord Alfreton had presented her with a gift, she had been sure he was going to propose. The soft silk of her dress spilling over her legs, with the ermine trim warming her neck. But instead, he pressed a small gift box into her palm, gave a perfunctory peck on the cheek, his clammy skin barely brushing hers, and informed her he was ending their courtship to marry Lady Priscilla Merryweather instead - a woman of greater means and status.

Daphne had stumbled back in shock, tears filling her eyes blurring her vision. Lord Alfreton offered a few empty words of apology before disappearing back into the ball, leaving her utterly heartbroken. She had fled home early, flinging the unopened gift box into a drawer in her desk.

After that she refused to see Lord Alfreton again, unable to bear the pain. From then on, anything that reminded Daphne of the holidays only brought back the bitter sting of Lord Alfreton's betrayal. Christmas became an endless source of sadness. Every carol and Christmas hymn she recalled singing off tune with Alfreton. She remembered shared glances over the rims of cups of wassail. The smell of cinnamon and pine evoking thoughts of shared laughter and tender handholding.

The present-day ballroom swirled back into focus as the painful memories receded. Daphne straightened her posture, reinforcing her defences against Christmas sentimentality. She would not be hurt so easily ever again.

As she brooded in the corner, Daphne didn't notice the handsome stranger staring at her from across the room. He made his way through the crowd and introduced himself with a deep bow.

'My apologies for not waiting for a proper introduction. Duke of Hazelbury, at your service. And you are?'

'Edward?' Daphne gasped; her nose wrinkled in surprise. The man before Daphne stood tall at good six feet, his chiselled features slightly tanned and his eyes piercingly blue, a far cry from the short pudgy boy who had followed her older brother around. 'My, how you've changed! I think you and I might have a chance against my brother and cousin now in those snowball fights.' He looked so different, yet so familiar. The shy boy she once knew was now a handsome duke. She had not seen him in ten years, first, his grandfather had sent him to Eton then he had left for the continent. They had exchanged for some time, but his physical changes had not been conveyed through the pen.

'Daphne?' Edward's eyes widened 'I am not the only one who has changed. Why on earth are you wearing black? Have I missed a death?' Edward frowned.

'Only that of my Christmas spirit, I am afraid.' Daphne could not help but smile for the first time that night.

Two

Chapter 2

Daphne shook her head, bitterness creeping into her voice. 'Christmas holds no joy for me now. The holidays only bring heartache.'

'Not if I have any say in the matter.' Edward gave her a cocky grin. 'Daphne, do you remember the snowball fights we used to have with James, Sophie and Cousin Michael? Sledging down the hills behind the manor? Carolling in the village square? I do not care what has happened to you since I last heard from you, I think I shall set myself the goal of bringing you Christmas cheer again.'

In spite of herself, Daphne felt her lips curve into a small smile at the memories. 'The five of us were quite the troublemakers.'

'Exactly!' Edward grinned. 'And we're going to make trouble again. I'm going to remind you just how magical Christmas can be.'

Daphne searched his face. Perhaps she had been too quick to dismiss the season. With Edward here, she felt the first stirrings of Christmas spirit within her heart.

'Well,' she said slowly. 'I suppose we could try.'

Edward laughed and pulled her into the swirling waltz that was being played, spinning around the ballroom. The candles seemed to glow brighter as Daphne laughed. She had missed Edward more than she realised. A heat began to build in her chest, thawing her frozen heart just a little. Maybe this Christmas would be different after all.

* * *

Across the ballroom, Sophie noticed Daphne's improved spirits as she danced with Edward. Delighted to see her sister finally smiling again, Sophie turned to the man beside her. 'Forgive me, I don't believe we've been introduced. I'm Lady Sophie Brookshire, the younger Brookshire sister.' She curtsied prettily, ignoring propriety in introducing herself to the quiet man.

The red-haired man bowed awkwardly. 'Lord Thistleson, Nigel, at your service.' He fumbled over his words, cheeks flushing. 'That is…I arrived with Hazelbury. The new Duke of Hazelbury I mean.'

Sophie smiled warmly. 'We were childhood friends.' She tilted her head. 'Will you be staying in the area long?'

'Oh, um, yes. As long as Hazelbury remains.' Nigel stared at his shoes.

Taking pity on his bashfulness, Sophie said gently, 'Well, I do hope you'll join us for Christmas dinner. Cook is simply the best. And I am assuming that you and Hazelbury would be alone otherwise.'

Nigel finally met her eyes, relief crossing his face. 'You are too kind, Lady Sophie. I should like that very much.'

They shared a smile. Though Nigel remained reserved, Sophie sensed a sincerity about him. As lively music filled the air, she found herself wishing the night would never end. 'My lady, would you do the honour of dancing this cotillion with me?' Nigel extended a hand. He clumsily guided her out onto the floor, his cheeks flushing when he bumped into her shoulder.

After finishing the lively cotillion with Nigel, Sophie fanned herself and turned cheerfully to chat with her friends. 'Emma! How delightful to see you.' She air-kissed her childhood friend. 'That gown is simply divine on you. I love the length of the sleeves.'

As the two caught up on society gossip, Sophie's gaze occasionally strayed across the room to the awkward, yet endearing figure of Nigel. She felt her cheeks warm whenever their eyes happened to meet.

Later, as Nigel brought Sophie a cup of wassail, he hesitated before offering his arm. 'Would you care to take a turn about the room with me?'

'I would be delighted,' Sophie replied.

* * *

'Sister, you're practically glowing,' Daphne remarked as Sophie returned to her side. 'I do not think I've seen you smile so much all season.'

Sophie blushed. 'Lord Thistleson is a perfect gentleman. And so very thoughtful.' She glanced over at Nigel shyly.

Daphne followed her gaze. 'He seems a good match for you. I am happy to see you enjoying the festivities.' Her expression turned solemn. 'I know I have not been the most cheerful company of late.'

'Oh Daphne.' Sophie squeezed her hand. 'I understand why this time of year is difficult for you. But perhaps there is still room for Christmas magic?'

Daphne sighed, her eyes downcast. 'I lost faith in magic long ago. The holidays only remind me of what I have lost.'

'You have not lost everything,' Sophie said gently. 'We still have each other. And now Edward has returned, just when you needed him most.'

Daphne blinked back tears, conflicted emotions warring within her. 'I missed him more than I realised. Or maybe I missed the carefree way we were as children. But the past cannot be undone.' She touched the black fabric of her gown. 'Some wounds never fully heal.'

Sophie's face fell. 'If you cannot let go of the pain, it will swallow what joy remains. Do not let Alfreton steal your Christmas too.'

Daphne pondered her sister's words. Perhaps Sophie was right. Holding onto bitterness would only hurt them both. She had shut out the world for too long. It was time to start living again.

Daphne took a deep breath as she watched the dancers twirling across the ballroom floor. The music swelled around her, violins and cellos blending in joyful harmony. She used to love evenings like this, when the ballrooms filled with light and laughter.

Part of her longed to join in the festivities, to let the rhythm pull her into a waltz, Edward's strong hand clasping hers. But a deeper fear held her back, the icy chill of heartbreak not yet thawed.

She caught Edward gazing at her from across the room, his brilliant blue eyes alight with hope. He believed he could reignite her Christmas spirit, return her to the girl she used to be. But the intervening years had changed them both. The loss she suffered had left scars. Could she trust again, make herself vulnerable? Was Christmas magic powerful enough to heal old wounds?

Daphne wavered, emotions seesawing. Joy beckoned, whispering promises of new beginnings. Sorrow clung to her still, its barbed edges sharp and familiar. She teetered on the fulcrum between past and future, light and dark.

The choice was hers. She could stubbornly remain in the cold shadows, keeping her heart under lock and key. Or she could take a leap of faith, embrace hope's flickering flame once more.

Edward approached; hand extended in invitation. 'Dance with me.' His eyes pleaded, 'As a friend, let me show you that Christmastide is not as bad as it seems.'

Daphne trembled inside; tears threatened. Then slowly, she reached out and took his hand. The music swelled as they stepped onto the dance floor together.

Daphne floated across the polished parquet floor, Edward's strong arm encircling her waist. The strains of the violin soared as they whirled through the steps of the dance.

For a moment, she was transported back to gilded Christmas balls of the past, when hope and magic infused the season. Laughter once again rang out clear as bells, joyful as carollers.

Edward gazed down at her, his eyes twin beacons shining through the fog of her malaise. 'There is the Daphne I remember,' he murmured. 'The light in your eyes could make even the grumpiest curmudgeon smile.'

Heat rose in Daphne's cheeks. She had forgotten the power of Edward's flattery. A witty retort formed on her lips but softened into a smile. She gave his hand a grateful squeeze.

As the final notes faded, Edward bowed. 'May I have the honour of another dance, my lady? I know it is more than the allowed two, but, alas as we are in the country and there seems to be a dearth of interesting and eligible ladies. I am sure your father would not begrudge me one more given the smile upon your face.'

***

Daphne and Edward whirled around the dance floor, lost in lively conversation and reminiscence. Nearby, Nigel hovered awkwardly at the edge of the crowd, transfixed by Sophie's radiant smile as she laughed with friends. Mustering his courage, Nigel approached with a stiff bow. 'Lady Sophie, would you do me the honour of the next dance?' His face flushed as red as a poinsettia. 'I know a second dance may not be proper given we just met, but there seems to be a lack of female...' Sophie had not thought it possible but Nigel's face went an even deeper shade of red as Nigel tried the same line he had heard Edward use.

Sophie turned, surprised but clearly delighted. 'Why, of course, Lord Thistleson! Here is my dance card.'

When they took their positions, Sophie gave him an encouraging smile. Nigel straightened his shoulders and led her confidently into the steps. Soon they were gliding across the floor, Sophie's golden curls bouncing gently to the rhythm. Though Nigel remained quiet, his initial shyness was replaced by a glowing admiration and attentiveness to his lovely partner. Sophie's eyes sparkled as she drew him into a friendly conversation about life in the countryside, coaxing shy details from the reticent Nigel.

When the dance ended, they lingered a moment, hands clasped. Nigel bowed respectfully over Sophie's hand. 'Thank you for the dance, Lady Sophie. It was a pleasure to make your acquaintance.'

Sophie blushed prettily. 'The pleasure was all mine, Lord Thistleson.' As he retreated, she watched his tall frame disappear into the crowd, intrigued by this gentle soul.

***

Across the room, Daphne observed the exchange with a knowing smile. It seemed Christmas magic was weaving its spell on more than one lonely heart tonight.

As the evening wore on, Daphne found her mood slowly lifting. Edward's playful banter and reminiscing of their shared childhood brought a warmth to her heart she had not felt in years. He coaxed her to take a turn about the room with him; she laughed freely for the first time since Alfreton's betrayal.

When the clock chimed midnight, Edward drew her out onto the moonlit balcony. Daphne shivered as the cold night air hit her, the thin silk doing little to warm her. Noticing her discomfort, Edward removed his jacket and draped it around her. She clutched it tightly, surrounding herself in his warmth and woodsy scent.

'Daphne,' he said gently, 'I know Christmas may never be the same for you again. But I want you to know that it does not always have to be a time for solemnity.' He tilted her chin up to meet his earnest gaze. 'If you will let me, I would like to call on you and show you some of our old fun.'

Daphne's eyes glistened with unshed tears. 'Thank your grace,' she whispered. 'I think I'd like that very much.'

As snowflakes began to fall, Edward drew her close. Daphne rested her head on his chest, listening to the steady beat of his heart.

This Christmas would be different, she realised. The season of rebirth and new beginnings was upon her at last. As they stood there in the moonlit silence, Daphne felt a strange pull towards Edward. It was as though they were connected by an invisible thread, and no matter how hard she tried to resist it, the pull only grew stronger. She could feel his steady breaths on the top of her head, his chest rising and falling in a steady rhythm.

Daphne lifted her head, her eyes meeting Edward's. In that moment, she knew that he felt the same way she did. They leaned in towards each other, their lips meeting in a soft, tentative kiss. A jolt of electricity shot through Daphne's body as their lips touched, igniting a fire within her that she had thought long extinguished.

For a moment, they were lost in their own little world, the snow falling softly around them like a blanket. It was as though time had stopped, and they were the only two people left in the world.

As they broke the kiss, however, reality came crashing back. Daphne felt a sudden wave of panic wash over her as she realised what had just happened. She stepped back abruptly, her face flooding with embarrassment. What had come over her? How could she have let herself get so carried away? The last time she had been so foolish, Lord Alfreton had taken advantage and ultimately broken her heart.

Daphne was filled with dread as she realised that someone may have seen them from the ballroom window. Quickly, she passed Edward back his coat, bobbing a curtsy, she rushed back inside before anyone could notice her absence. As she made her way through the throng of guests, a sense of fear and guilt surged through her body. She was unwilling to open her heart again at Christmas time - it had already caused too much pain and anguish in the past. Despite Edward's kind words, Daphne knew it would be best to guard her heart from now on, no matter how kind or understanding he seemed to be.

Three

Chapter 3

❧

The carriage jostled over the snow-covered road, its wooden wheels crunching on the icy ruts. Daphne gazed out the frosted window, her breath fogging the glass.

'Oh, will it not be simply magical?' Sophie clasped her mittens in delight. 'Sipping wassail by the fireside as carols are sung. And the ballroom will glitter with candles and garlands!'

Daphne sighed, her melancholy unmatched by Sophie's cheer. 'I suppose.'

'You must not be a curmudgeon, dear sister. Why, I hear Lord Alfreton himself may be in attendance!'

A teasing smile turned Sophie's rosy cheeks even rosier. Daphne straightened in her seat. That insufferable cad, here? She clenched her jaw. If he dared speak to her… 'Do not vex me so, Sophie,' she chided, though a hint of amusement touched her voice. 'You know well my feelings on the matter.'

'Of course, of course.' Sophie waved a mittened hand. 'But one must hold out hope during this festive time! Perhaps you shall find it again, my dear.'

Daphne gazed out at the snow-cloaked firs passing by. 'Perhaps,' she murmured. But her heart remained dormant as the barren winter earth.

'Sophie dear. Do not pester your sister with talk of that awful man. Sit straighter, you will rumple your dress slouched like that.' Lady Jane fussed at her daughter's skirts. 'James, move over slightly so Sophie has room to move.'

'Mother, dearest. If you did not insist that my sisters wear a ridiculous number of layers there would be ample room in the coach for all five of us. As it is, father looks like he is almost hanging out the door.' James ducked a blow from his mother's fan.

'The boy's right Jane, if the girl's skirts get bigger, I'm going to have to lose some weight to ensure we fit. Or maybe we can stick James up top with the footman?' Lord Brookshire quirked an eyebrow.

'Father, if it was summer, I would be up there now, rather than stuck in here with a woman who beats me with a fan.' James eyed his mother's fan.

'Oh, you insufferable child!' Lady Jane looked offended before breaking into laughter. Soon the entire carriage was filled with mirth. 'It will be nice to see Edward, I mean His Grace, again.' She sighed. 'It is going to take some getting used to, calling him His Grace. In my mind, he is still a little boy who always seemed to have dirt on his nose.'

The carriage rolled to a stop before the grand arched doors of Jasper Park. Liveried footmen hustled forth, unfolding steps and opening creaking doors to help the ladies disembark.

Daphne gathered her skirts, stepping down into the softly falling snow. The icy flakes kissed her cheeks with cold whispers. She shivered, drawing her ermine-lined cloak tighter.

Sophie hopped down behind her, clapping her hands in delight. 'Oh, is it not perfectly picturesque!'

Daphne followed her sister's gaze. Beyond the carriage, glowing lamps lit an avenue of snow-frosted trees that led back towards the gate. In the distance, strains of harpsichord music and laughter drifted on the night air.

Arm in arm, the sisters walked up the lamp-lit path, boots crunching through the fresh powder, their parents and James following behind, still arguing over the fan. As they drew nearer, the music swelled - a chorus of voices raised in song.

'While Shepherds Watched Their Flocks at Night...'

Daphne tensed, the carol piercing her melancholy. She paused, blinking

17

back an old, familiar ache. Fear welled in her stomach.

Sophie gave her arm a gentle squeeze. 'Come, let us get you warm by the fire.'

With a brave swallow, Daphne nodded and allowed herself to be led towards the welcoming golden glow of Jasper Park.

Inside, the entrance hall blazed with warmth and light. Garlands of holly and evergreen wound up the grand staircase, filling the air with notes of pine and cinnamon. Servants bustled to and fro bearing trays of wassail and rum-laced eggnog.

Sophie eagerly shed her cloak, handing it to a waiting footman. She turned to Daphne with a pleading look. 'May I?'

Daphne nodded, watching as her sister hurried off to join the lively party. She moved slowly, drinking in the sights and sounds that assaulted her senses. The crackling fire, the rich scents, the peals of laughter - they flooded her with bittersweet nostalgia.

With a weary sigh, she wandered towards the back of the hall, avoiding the boisterous crowds. A set of French doors opened onto a moonlit terrace and the still, silent gardens beyond. Daphne stepped outside, welcoming the cold kiss of night air.

Her breath plumed before her as she followed a gravel path lined with dormant rose bushes, now just thorny tangles beneath their blanket of snow. She walked aimlessly, losing herself in memories of childhood Christmases long ago.

Skating on the frozen pond, singing carols round the piano, waking at dawn to unwrap presents. She remembered running through Jasper Park, chasing Edward and James while her parents had called upon the previous Duke Hazelbury. Joys now faded into the distant past. Lost in reminiscence, Daphne did not notice the dark clouds rolling in, nor the thickening of the softly falling snow. Not until the flurries turned to swirling white and the wind began to howl through the barren garden.

She glanced up in surprise as icy gusts lashed at her cloak. The manor house was no longer in sight, obscured by the mounting blizzard. Daphne shivered, filled with sudden dread. Which way had she come?

Daphne turned in circles, searching in vain for some familiar landmark or glimmer of light amid the featureless snow and skeletal bushes. She was well and truly lost. The wind tore at her like icy claws, snowflakes stinging her cheeks.

Just as panic threatened to seize her, a light appeared through the storm's fury, drawing closer. Daphne squinted, making out a tall figure holding a lantern. She gasped as he came into view.

'Lady Daphne!' Edward exclaimed, surprise in his tone. 'What are you doing out in this weather? . Lord Wintershire said he thought he had seen someone head out into the garden. With this weather, I thought it best to check.'

Daphne bit back a sharp retort, her teeth chattering violently. 'I went for a walk. Got turned around.'

His gaze softened with understanding. Wordlessly, he removed his coat and draped it around her shaking shoulders. Daphne clutched at its warmth, the scent of sandalwood enveloping her. The storm lashed its fury at them.

'Come, there is a greenhouse just ahead. We will take shelter there.' Edward guided her firmly forwards with the light, a beacon through the swirling chaos.

They stumbled inside, snow spraying behind them. The air was humid, earthy with the smell of soil and greenery. Vines curled around the glass walls, exotic flowers nodding in the draft.

Daphne sank onto a stone bench, breathless. She felt suddenly shy, unsure what to say. Awkward silence stretched between them. The knowledge that they were alone, unchaperoned weighed heavily on them.

After a moment, Edward gestured to a potted plant. 'Hellebores. Your favourite, if I recall?'

Daphne nodded, a hint of a smile touching her lips. 'We had them in the garden at home.' She reached out and gently brushed the drooping blooms, remembering. The memories came flooding back - of her and Edward as children, playing hide-and-seek amid the flowers. So long ago, yet still vivid in her mind.

Daphne's fingers lingered on the hellebore's petals, her eyes growing distant.

'I used to love this time of year,' she murmured. 'Carolling, baking gingerbread, the smell of pine in every room.' Her voice caught. 'It hasn't felt the same since...' She trailed off, but Edward seemed to understand. He sat beside her on the bench, hands folded, listening intently. 'You were away when I met Lord Alfreton.' Daphne blinked back tears, keeping her gaze fixed on the flowers.

'I honestly thought he loved me.' She gave a sad little laugh. 'He thought the Yuletide ball was a good place to tell me he was marrying Pricilla Merryweather.'

Edward nodded; his eyes full of compassion. 'Heartbreak makes the holidays difficult. The contrast between joy and sorrow...'

'Yes, exactly.' Daphne's shoulders relaxed slightly. It was a relief to finally voice her feelings to someone who understood.

'With time, perhaps you can find a way to forget him while also embracing new traditions.' Edward's voice was gentle. 'Do not lose hope this season can bring happiness again.' He brushed a stray tendril of hair away from her face, his hand warm against her chilled cheek.

Daphne managed a small, grateful smile. For the first time in years, she felt a glimmer of Christmas spirit stirring within.

* * *

Sophie glided through the grand hall, humming 'God rest ye merry gentlemen' under her breath. Garlands of holly and mistletoe adorned the walls, filling the room with the fresh scent of pine.

She spotted Nigel standing alone near the fireplace, fidgeting with his gloves. His eyes followed Sophie as she checked on the hot cider and helped a servant hang the last of the stockings.

'There, now it's perfect!' Sophie beamed, stepping back to admire her handywork. Nigel opened his mouth as if to speak, then seemed to think better of it and stared down at his shoes. Sophie breezed over to him. 'Happy Christmas, my lord! Are you enjoying the party?'

'Oh! Um, yes, quite...' Nigel's face flushed as red as the poinsettias. He snuck a glance at Sophie's radiant smile. 'You look lovely.'

'Why, thank you.' Sophie met his shy gaze. 'Would you care to join me for some singing? I could use a partner.'

'I'm not much of a singer.' Nigel rubbed his neck, looking ready to bolt.

'Nonsense, anyone can sing at Christmas.' Sophie gently took his arm. 'Just follow my lead.'

As they sang 'God rest ye merry gentlemen' Nigel finally relaxed. His tentative baritone blended pleasingly with Sophie's soprano. A few party guests turned their heads, smiling at the unlikely duo.

Sophie gave Nigel's arm an encouraging squeeze. For an instant, their eyes locked and held. Sophie's heart fluttered at the warmth in Nigel's expression. Perhaps her patience was starting to pay off.

* * *

Meanwhile, trapped in the greenhouse, Edward paced while Daphne sat staring at an Espalier apple tree, lost in thought. She barely noticed when Edward approached and took the seat beside her.

'Beautiful tree,' he commented. 'Though not quite as grand as the ones at Brookshire Manor.'

Daphne glanced up, startled from her reverie. 'Yes, nothing compared to the thirty-foot trees in the orchards.' A wistful look crossed her face. 'Do you remember when Cook would hoist us up to sneak a fresh apple? I was always terrified of falling.'

Edward chuckled. 'And I always volunteered to catch you.'

'My gallant hero. And in winter we would build snow forts throughout the orchard.' Daphne's lips quirked. She gazed into the fire once more, her smile fading. 'Christmas was always my favourite. But now...'

'Now it only brings heartache,' Edward finished gently.

Daphne turned to him, unshed tears glistening. 'I miss those days. The carols, the feasts, the magic. It's all gone because of one sentence.'

Edward hesitated, then laid a comforting hand over hers. 'Perhaps the magic lies within us, waiting to be rekindled.' His fingers laced with hers.

Daphne searched his earnest eyes. For a moment, she allowed herself to reminisce, sharing stories of Christmas mornings long ago, when joy had filled her heart to the brim. Butterflies stirred in her stomach, the heat of his hand on hers coupled with the thought of the past making her feel content for the second time that season.

Daphne found herself getting lost in the memories, momentarily transported back to happier times. She told Edward about the Christmas pantomimes she and Sophie used to put on, staying up all night to make costumes out of old curtains and bedsheets. She described the candlelit midnight mass, the hushed splendour of the church decked with garlands of fir and yew. Her voice grew warm as she recalled the smell of cinnamon and cloves wafting from the kitchens, the sound of laughter from the parlour, and the feel of new-fallen snow beneath her boots.

Edward listened intently. He interjected now and then with his own recollections - the clatter of the horses' hooves trotting through the snow, the bitter chill of the ice-skating pond and the glowing candles in the hallway reflected in her eyes. With each shared memory, he saw the hardness in Daphne's expression soften, her manner losing its guard. For the first time in the last two years, she felt a tendril of Christmas joy unfurling within her heart.

***

Back in the ballroom room, Sophie smiled encouragingly at Nigel as he haltingly described the yuletide customs of his home. 'After my mother died, I was sent to live with her sister in Saalfeld. My aunt, Augusta and my cousin, Sophie,' He smiled at the name connection. 'They would decorate this wonderful pine tree with dried fruit and nuts.' Though shy at first, he gradually opened up, made bold by the kindness in her eyes. Their conversation meandered from topic to topic - carols, holiday foods, gift-giving traditions. With each new subject Nigel's speech grew more fluid, more relaxed.

When Sophie laughed at one of his dry, awkward jokes, a glimmer of pride and affection shone through Nigel's diffidence. Their gazes held for a moment too long before Sophie demurely dropped her eyes with a blush. Both felt the delicate thread drawing them together; a new understanding blossomed like the first unfurling of a poinsettia's crimson leaves.

* * *

Daphne glanced out the frost-laced window, a furrow of worry creasing her brow. Though she had allowed herself to feel joy this night, she knew heartache still awaited in the days to come. The past could wound, but it could also heal - if one had the courage to face it.

'Looks like the storm is dying down a bit. I think we are going to have to chance it.' Edward lifted the lantern and helped guide Daphne to the door. 'Come, at least I am pretty sure I know the way back to the house.' The two of them ran through the winding pathways back to the house. They slipped several times on the ice forming on the paths, hanging onto one another and laughing.

Sophie felt Nigel's shy touch on her arm as he excused himself from their circle of conversation. She watched him exit, a pensive look on her face. What future might they have, with the differences in their stations? She the daughter of a Marquis and he the son of… well she was not sure, the name Thistleson was not known to her. But she was an optimist at heart - she had to believe that love would find a way.

She heard a door click and Daphne and Edward slid into the house, shaking snow from their hair and cloaks. Hurriedly, she raced over, looped her arm through her sister's and drew her away before anyone else noticed. 'Daphne! Where have you been! I assumed you were skulking somewhere quiet and out of the way, not running around in a snowstorm with Lord Hazelbury!'

'I went for a walk in the gardens and got caught in the storm. His Grace found me, and we took refuge in a greenhouse.' Daphne stomped her feet in an attempt to warm them.

'Alone?' Sophie gasped.

'Yes alone. But shush, nothing happened. Just some reminiscing and thought pondering.' Daphne flexed her gloved fingers. 'Where is mother and father? I assume we will be heading home now. It looks like the party is ending.'

'There you girls are!' Lady Jane swept into view. 'Come now the sleigh awaits. Your father and James are already inside and arguing over seating arrangements. Thank goodness the driver had the foresight to head home and swap out the carriage for the sleigh. What an awful snow storm. I feel sorry for the Hazelbury housekeeper, I am sure there will be many people staying tonight. I am also sure there may be more than one engagement to come of it.'

Four

Chapter 4

The snow fell in heavy swaths, blanketing the rolling hills in a pristine coat of white. Crystalline flakes clung to the bare tree limbs and settled atop the frozen pond, transforming the once vibrant gardens into a still wintry landscape.

Daphne stood solemnly by the frosted window, staring out at the silent expanse. She shivered as a draft crept through Brookshire manor, the cold seeping into her bones. Behind her, the crackling fire did little to warm the perpetual chill in her heart.

'Daphne!' Edward's voice rang out brightly as he bounded into the parlour, rubbing his gloved hands together in anticipation. 'The sleigh is ready. Are you looking forward to our ride?'

Daphne turned, forcing a small smile. 'I suppose a short ride would provide a diverting amusement.'

Edward's grin faltered slightly. 'Come now, do not be like that. I know how you used to love racing through the snowdrifts when we were children.' He paused, his expression softening. 'I thought perhaps it might help restore some of the Christmas spirit you seem to have lost.'

Daphne tensed, old wounds rising to the surface. Lord Alfreton's betrayal

25

had snuffed out her joy like a candle in the wind. She had not celebrated properly since, the familiar carols only deepening her melancholy.

'Forgive me,' she said quietly. 'I feel out of sorts today. But I appreciate you trying to rekindle those memories.'

Edward stepped closer; his eyes filled with empathy. 'I understand. My hope is that we may create new memories together…as more than friends.' He held out his hand.

Daphne hesitated, then placed her hand in his, allowing him to lead her out to begin their sleigh ride. Perhaps with Edward's patience and compassion, she could find her Christmas spirit once more.

The horses' hooves clip-clopped steadily on the blanket of fresh snow, their breath forming misty plumes in the cold winter air. Daphne pulled her woollen shawl tighter around her shoulders as the sleigh glided over the pristine white hills bordering the estate. Though initially reluctant, she soon found herself mesmerised by the peaceful beauty surrounding them. Icicles hung from the bare tree branches, sparkling like diamonds when they passed through sunbeams peeking through the clouds. The bitter chill nipped at Daphne's cheeks, but she hardly noticed, enthralled by the tranquil scene.

Beside her, Edward studied Daphne's features, delighted to see the creases in her brow smooth and a softness return to her eyes. 'I'd nearly forgotten how lovely the grounds look at Christmastime,' he remarked. 'Remember when we were children, and you convinced me to have a snowball fight inside the house? Your father was furious when he saw the mess in the foyer!'

Daphne couldn't help but chuckle at the memory. 'And Cook made us hot cocoa to warm up afterward, with marzipan sweets.' A wistful sigh escaped her lips. 'I miss those simpler times.' Next to Daphne, Helena, along to be chaperone but pretending not to be there, made a snorting sound as she tried not to laugh at the thought of Cook encouraging the bad behaviour.

'As do I,' Edward said gently. 'But we can make new memories, Daphne. Ones filled with the same joy and laughter we knew back then.'

Daphne turned to him, her eyes glistening. Perhaps it was time to let go of the past hurts and look ahead to the promise of a new year, with Edward's friendship lighting the way.

Daphne looked down, picking at a loose thread on her glove. 'You're right, of course. It's only…' She hesitated, a pained expression flitting across her face.

Edward leaned forward, his eyes searching hers with concern. 'What is it, Daphne? You know you can tell me anything.'

She nodded slowly, taking a shaky breath. 'It's just…ever since Lord Alfreton,' She made a wave gesture. 'I've struggled to feel that same Christmas spirit I once had. His betrayal broke something in me.' Daphne blinked back tears, ashamed to show such vulnerability.

'I understand,' Edward said gently. 'A wound like that does not heal easily. But you have so much strength in you, Daphne. And people who care deeply for your happiness.' He reached for her hand, giving it a reassuring squeeze.

Daphne allowed herself a small smile, comforted by his words. For a moment, looking into his earnest eyes, she felt a glimmer of hope. Perhaps this Christmas could be different…

But then the icy fingers of doubt clutched at her heart again. She pulled her hand away, the walls going up around her once more. 'Forgive me, I should not have said anything. Let us just focus on enjoying the ride.' Daphne straightened in her seat, staring straight ahead as she retreated into herself. The sleigh bells jingled merrily, oblivious to her inner turmoil.

Edward studied her with concern but did not press the matter further. They continued on in silence through the snow-blanketed meadows, the space between them suddenly feeling very wide.

Edward let out a small sigh, his breath clouding in the frosty air. He understood Daphne's need to protect her heart, but it pained him to see her shut him out again.

'Daphne,' he began gently, 'I know you have been deeply hurt. But please know that I only wish for your happiness. Our friendship means the world to me.'

Daphne continued staring ahead, though her stoic facade flickered slightly at his words.

'We have built a great deal of trust over the years,' Edward continued. 'I hope you know that you can always confide in me, about anything. I would never betray your confidence or take advantage of your vulnerabilities. You are far too dear to me for that.'

At this, Daphne finally turned to meet his earnest gaze. The icy wall around her heart began to thaw ever so slightly. She wanted to believe his assurances, to give in to the comfort and understanding he offered.

Yet the bitter scars left by Lord Alfreton made it difficult to let her guard down fully. What if she bared her soul to Edward, only to have him turn his back as well? Could her battered heart endure being shattered once more? Daphne wavered, torn between a longing for human connection and a desperate need for self-preservation. Edward's patience and empathy kindled a fragile ember of hope within her, yet fear's icy grip remained strong.

'Do you know how annoying you are by being so dower all the time? Must you continue to brood even during such a festive outing?' Edward turned to glare at Daphne, keeping one hand on the reins. 'I care a lot about you Daphne. I hate to see you so.'

'I did not ask you to try to make me happy. I was more than comfortable trying to avoid all holiday cheer.' Daphne straightened her spine.

'That may be so, but you make everyone else around you miserable in the process!' Edward's face flushed with frustration as he continued, 'I mean only to share merriment with a dear friend, but you rebuff me at every turn, fixated on past griefs. Pray stop being so pig-headed and see what is right before you!'

'Ay, Your Grace! Look out!' Helena squealed from her seat next to Daphne. Distracted by their argument, Edward did not notice the path ahead taking a perilous turn. A massive oak, felled by winter storms, lay across their route, obscured by drifting snow. Edward pulled sharply on the reins but too late— the sleigh's runner clouted the log with a violent crack. Thrown from his seat, Edward landed in a powdery snowdrift.

'Whoa there!' Daphne called out, seizing the flapping reins as the startled horse threatened to bolt. With soothing words, she gently brought the animal under control, halting the sleigh's careening progress. Its runner was badly splintered but still attached.

Edward rose gingerly from the bank, snow clinging to his hat and coat.

'Well done, Daphne,' he moved to calm the horses. 'Your quick action spared us from a worse fate. Are you both alright?' He looked at the two women still inside the sleigh. Helena gave a slight nod, her face an ashen white.

Daphne flashed him a relieved smile. 'It seems you have survived with just a bruised pride. Shall we assess the damage and attempt to limp back home?'

Edward nodded and took up the reins again, keeping a watchful eye for obstacles ahead. With Daphne's steady presence, they slowly turned the sleigh around, the ruined runner scraping along. Edward's carelessness had nearly spoiled their outing, but Daphne's poise in a crisis helped avert disaster.

'My apologies Daphne.' Edward concentrated on the path home. 'Had I not raised my voice, I would have seen our predicament.'

'I fail to see how one's voice and one's eyes are connected.' Daphne gave Edward a slight grin. Her heart was still pounding from the incident. She could not bear to think of Edward being hurt. Heat began to rise in her cheeks as she realised that she had come to care about the Duke of Hazelbury as more than a friend. They managed to return to the manor without further incident.

As Daphne grappled internally, Sophie's airy laughter rang out from the parlour. Daphne walked in the door to see her younger sister seated at the pianoforte, smiling warmly as she encouraged Thistleson to join her in a duet.

'Oh, come now, Lord Thistleson, you simply must share those musical talents Edward boasts of,' Sophie cajoled playfully.

Nigel flushed crimson, rubbing his neck as he hemmed and hawed. 'Oh, well, I'm not sure...' he stammered, nearly tripping over his own feet as he backed away.

Sophie tinkled a few notes on the piano keys. 'Please my lord? For me?' She smiled winningly up at him with a flutter of her lashes.

'I-I suppose one song couldn't hurt,' Nigel relented bashfully. He settled onto the pianoforte bench beside Sophie, keeping a careful distance between them.

Sophie began playing a cheerful Christmas melody, keeping the tempo slow. Nigel joined in hesitantly, his long fingers moving clumsily over the keys at first. Yet as the song went on, his playing became surer and more confident.

Daphne watched the pair, a bittersweet mix of emotions welling within her. She was happy to see Sophie's infectious warmth thawing Nigel's shy reserve. Yet their blossoming connection accentuated her own detachment and loneliness.

As the song ended, Sophie playfully bumped her shoulder against Nigel's. 'See, that was not so frightening after all!'

Nigel ducked his head, rubbing his neck again sheepishly. 'I suppose not. You have a gift for putting me at ease, Lady Sophie.'

Sophie's eyes sparkled. 'Please, call me Sophie.'

Nigel nodded, flushing once more. 'Sophie,' he repeated softly, as if trying out the sweet sound of her name.

Sophie stood, smoothing out her dress. 'Come, let's see if Mrs. Potter has any spiced cider ready.' She extended her hand towards Nigel in invitation.

He took it gingerly, nearly stumbling again in his haste to stand. Sophie caught his arm to steady him, amusement dancing in her eyes. Sophie's maid rose from her chair in the corner, placing some mending to the side.

Arm in arm, the two made their way towards the kitchens, leaving Daphne to observe their departing figures pensively. Perhaps if she could relinquish her bitterness like Sophie, she too could find a second chance at love. For now, it remained out of reach, but hope was beginning to ignite within her heart once more.

Turning away, she moved to the window and gazed out at the gently falling snow. The pure white blanket softened the edges of the world, muffling sound and blurring shapes into hazy impressions. It was a landscape of new beginnings, of possibilities not yet explored.

Moving upstairs to her bedroom, Daphne opened her dresser drawer and drew out the gift Alfreton had pressed into her hand before breaking her heart.

With hesitant steps, she moved to her sitting room where she sat with the gift, running her fingers over the smooth wrapping before carefully undoing the bow. The paper fell away to reveal an ornate box, which she lifted with slightly trembling hands. Nestled inside was a glass ornament in the shape of a bird.

Daphne's breath caught. She remembered the first time Lord Alfreton had given her a similar bird, hand-painted by a Venetian artisan. 'It reminded me of you,' he had said softly. 'Delicate but strong, and beautiful when taking flight.'

Now, staring at the glittering ornament, she felt the full force of emotions she had barricaded away for so long - grief, anger, and most of all, a yearning for the innocent joy and hope she had once felt.

With great care, Daphne lifted the bird from the box, turning it to catch the firelight. Then slowly, deliberately, she walked to the hearth and held it over the low flames...

Daphne hesitated, the ornament precariously close to the fire. The flames' heat licked at her fingers, yet still she could not release it.

'Daphne?'

She started at the sound of Edward's voice behind her. Turning, she saw his gaze move between her pained expression and the ornament.

'Forgive me, I didn't mean to intrude,' he said gently. 'Only, your sister said I might find you here.'

With sudden fury, she flung the ornament into the fiery grate. It shattered, fine glass dusting the logs.

Edward started forward, distraught. 'Daphne, I'm so sorry I didn't mean to startle you!'

Daphne turned to him, tears flowing freely now. 'Your Grace, no... Please, just go...' She tried to hide her tears. Edward brought up so many feelings but it was not his fault.

Edward hesitated, seeing the depth of Daphne's pain. Though it pained him, he knew she needed time alone.

'As you wish,' he said softly, indicating to Helena that she would not be needed as chaperone. 'But I am here as your friend, whenever you are ready.' He left her sitting room, mind churning with concern. The ornament breaking had clearly upset her - but it was just a trinket. Perhaps he could find a replacement to cheer her up.

Edward said farewell to James, ensured Nigel was alright to get home when he was finished paying attention to Lady Sophie, fetched his coat and headed into the village, the snow crunching under his boots. At the quaint Christmas market, he perused the artisan stalls until he found it - an ornament identical to the one Daphne had broken. Delicately wrought glass shaped like a bird, glittering in the winter sun.

He purchased it and tucked it safely in his pocket, imagining how Daphne's face would light up when he presented it to her. It was a small gesture, but one that would show his commitment to helping her find Christmas joy once again.

Humming a carol, Edward hurried back through the snowy landscape, heart swelling with care for his dear friend Daphne. He would remind her that the past need not darken the present - not when there was light and hope ahead.

Five

Chapter 5

The double doors to the drawing room creaked open and Edward entered, his boots sinking into the plush carpet. In his palms he cradled a small object wrapped in linen. 'Daphne, I have something for you,' he announced, crossing the room to stand before her.

Daphne set down her book, eyeing the bundle curiously. 'Oh?'

With a flourish, Edward unveiled a glittering glass bird ornament. Faceted crystal captured the light, sending rainbow prisms dancing over its outstretched wings.

Daphne's eyes widened in shock. She shrank back into her chair as if burned. 'This…this is in poor taste. Take it away at once,' she stammered.

Edward's grinning expression faltered. 'It is exactly like the one you broke yesterday. I saw how upset by it you were. Do you not like it?'

'Like it? I… I cannot bear to look upon it.' Daphne averted her gaze, distress etched across her face.

'Daphne, what is the matter?' Edward's voice was tinged with hurt. He stepped forward, extending the ornament.

Daphne held up a hand as if to ward him off. 'Please, just go.'

'At least tell me why. Have I caused offence?'

Daphne's eyes flashed with anger and pain. 'That was Lord Alfreton's gift to me that he pushed into my hands as he told me he did not love me. A crystal bird, this very style. When he cast me aside, I never opened it. That is, until yesterday. I... I smashed it in anger.'

Edward paled, shame flooding his face. 'Daphne, forgive me. I had no idea.'

Daphne turned away, tears shimmering in her eyes. The memories were too much to bear. She had no words, only a desperate desire for Edward to take his gift and leave her be.

Edward reached for her; palms open in supplication. 'Daphne, I swear, I did not know. I saw it in the market and thought it a perfect replica of your ornament.'

Daphne recoiled from his touch. 'You know nothing of my family's ornaments,' she hissed. Behind her careful composure, grief and anger roiled. How dare he presume such familiarity? This trinket was an insult to her loss. She had trusted him, allowed herself to hope, only to be betrayed again.

'Let me explain,' he implored, voice low and earnest. 'I wanted to find something to remind you of happier times, of the joy you have lost.'

Daphne searched his face, yearning to believe him even as doubt held her back. She saw only sincerity in his eyes. But the ornament's presence still cut deep, the pain too near.

'Please, Daphne,' he murmured. 'I never meant to cause you harm.' He reached for her hand, gentle yet resolute.

She wavered, tears blurring her vision. She wanted to cling to him, to the possibility of light in this darkest season. But the shadows of grief still gripped her heart.

Daphne pulled her hand away, the sting of his presumed deception still too fresh. 'I need time,' she said quietly, turning from him. She moved to the window, staring sightlessly at the snowy grounds. Behind her, she heard Edward sigh.

'I understand,' he said after a moment. 'Take all the time you need. But please know I care for you deeply, Daphne. I only want to see you smile again. As does your whole family, once I think you considered me part of that family.'

His words washed over her, equal parts balm and irritation. She resented his persistence even as her heart quickened at his confession.

'Do you remember when we first met?' Edward continued gently. 'James and Michael had found me playing alone at Jasper Park, my father had just died, and grandfather wanted me close.' He reached out and took her hand. 'We tried to call ourselves by our titles, as is proper, but we kept mucking it up, and we just started calling one another by first names. James introduced me to you, and you said Earl Greyson sounded like a good name for a type of tea. You demanded to be allowed to call me Edward like your brother. James said you could only call me Edward if you married me. You said maybe you would, one day.'

Despite herself, Daphne's lips quirked. She did remember. She had been very put out that she was not supposed to play with the boys.

'I should have told you then,' Edward went on, 'but you captivated me. Please do not shut me out now.'

Daphne gripped the windowsill until her knuckles whitened. She wanted to melt into his embrace, to leave the past behind. But its thorns still clung to her, unwilling to release their hold.

'Just go,' she whispered finally, eyes closed against the tears. 'Just ... go.'

She heard Edward sigh again, heavier this time. His retreating footsteps echoed her own heartbreak. Alone once more, Daphne wept.

As Daphne's melancholy deepened, her younger sister Sophie remained a ray of sunshine in the drafty manor. While Daphne isolated herself in her shadowy chambers, Sophie's voice fluttered down the hallway, humming cheerful snippets of carols. The scent of fir and tart cranberries followed Sophie as she flitted about, decorating the dark wood-panelled halls with bursts of festive greenery. Her wind-chapped cheeks glowed rosy in the candlelight as she stood back to admire her handywork, the glossy emerald leaves and scarlet berries glistening amidst the flurries swirling outside the frosted windowpanes.

In the parlour, she found Nigel staring contemplatively into the fire, seemingly oblivious to the cup of hot chocolate beside him. She heard Edward in the drawing room talking to Daphne. Sophie studied the gangly young man, whose thatch of coppery hair fell perpetually into his eyes. Though awkward in company, she had seen hints of a poetic soul beneath his shy exterior.

'Come help me finish decorating the fireplace,' Sophie said gently, holding out a string of popcorn.

Nigel started, broken from his reverie. 'Oh, I-I couldn't,' he stammered. 'These garlands require an artist's touch.'

Sophie smiled. 'Then an artist you shall be. Here.' She placed the popcorn in his hesitant hands and positioned them on the mantle. Nigel fumbled at first but soon fell into the rhythm of decoration.

As they worked, Sophie hummed "God Rest Ye Merry Gentlemen." Nigel paused to watch her, his cheeks colouring.

'You have a lovely voice,' he murmured.

'As do you,' Sophie said. 'Sing with me!'

'Oh no, I could not possibly—' Nigel protested, but Sophie began the melody again. Timidly he joined in, gaining confidence with each line. Their voices intertwined in imperfect harmony.

When the song ended, Nigel shyly presented Sophie with a lopsided woollen scarf. 'I made this for you,' he admitted. 'I know it is not much…'

'It is wonderful,' Sophie assured him. She wrapped the scarf around her neck, beaming. 'What a thoughtful gesture, thank you my lord. Knitting is an unusual past time for a lord.'

He flushed with pride and relief. 'My mother was ill for some time when I was a boy. She could not move from her bed. I had her teach me knitting and a bit of embroidery, just so I could spend more time with her since she could not play with me. My father hated it, probably one of the reasons he sent me away.' Sophie's heart swelled, even as she checked her instinct to throw her arms around him impulsively. Propriety must be maintained, though new feelings beckoned tantalizingly beneath the surface.

She sensed behind Nigel's formality a deep well of emotion he longed to express. In time, she hoped to gently coax it out of him. For now, patience and encouragement would see this tender bud blossom.

Heart pounding, Nigel opened his mouth to finally confess his feelings. But the words stuck in his throat. Sophie watched him expectantly, but he merely flushed deeper and turned away.

'Happy Christmas,' Nigel mumbled instead, internally cursing his cowardice. There would be other moments, he told himself. Other moments to share what beat so powerfully in his heart.

* * *

The cheerful sounds of Christmas preparation faded as Daphne wandered the manor's empty halls. She paused before the parlour, watching her younger sister Sophie laugh and sing carols with Nigel. Daphne's heart ached, remembering happier times decorating these same rooms with Lord Alfreton.

'There you are, darling.' Lady Jane's gentle voice broke Daphne's reverie. 'Your father and I have been looking for you.'

Daphne turned to face her parents, schooling her features into a facade of calm. 'Forgive me, I was merely...admiring the garlands.'

Lady Jane clasped Daphne's hands, her brow furrowing with concern. 'This melancholy does not suit you, my dear. I know the holidays are difficult.' She trailed off delicately.

Lord Brookshire cleared his throat. 'We cannot have you moping about the house. James mentioned the Wintershires are hosting a luncheon tomorrow. You should join him and your friends - it will do you good to get out amongst society.'

Daphne tensed, the thought of facing a crowd overwhelming. Sensing her reticence, Lady Jane added lightly, 'Perhaps you could accompany Sophie and Lord Thistleson, she will need a chaperone. I do believe they would make a charming pair, if he could but overcome his bashfulness.'

Despite herself, Daphne felt a flicker of amusement at her mother's matchmaking. 'You may be right, Mother. I shall...consider attending.'

Lady Jane kissed Daphne's cheek. 'That's my brave girl.'

As her parents left, Daphne turned back to the parlour. Through the garlanded doorway, she glimpsed Sophie adjusting her new lopsided scarf, her eyes soft. Daphne's own eyes pricked with tears. She slipped away before the merrymakers could notice, her hollow footsteps echoing down the corridor.

She needed air. Slipping into her wool coat, Daphne stepped out into the frozen gardens. Her breath misted before her as she followed the winding path to the frozen pond. Under the sun's wan light, the ice glimmered like flawed crystal.

Daphne stared down at her fractured reflection. Lord Alfreton's face swam before her mind's eye, his smile as he laughed with his new wife searing itself into her memory. She wrapped her arms around herself, overwhelmed by a fresh wave of heartache.

Sophie found Daphne standing solemnly by the frozen pond. 'Daphne, what are you doing out here?' she chided. 'Let's get you back inside before you catch cold.'

As they walked arm-in-arm back to the house, Sophie said gently, 'I know how difficult this season is for you. But you still have so much to hope for.'

When Daphne remained unconvinced, Sophie sighed. She longed to help her sister rediscover the magic of Christmas. An idea sparked. Perhaps she might embroider her black gowns she currently favoured, in festive red and green. At least that would bring some cheer while Edward worked to mend her broken heart.

Sophie resolved to set her plan in motion soon. She had always had a knack for bringing joy to others through little acts of kindness. Surely even Daphne's wounded spirit could not withstand such a loving Christmas surprise.

Daphne allowed Sophie to lead her back inside, though her heart felt like a lump of ice in her chest. The warmth of the hall enveloped her, yet she shivered, unable to shake off the chill of melancholy that had settled upon her spirit.

Out of the corner of her eye, she saw Edward approaching, his expression filled with concern. Daphne tensed, steeling herself for another well-meaning attempt to draw her out of her shell.

'Daphne,' Edward began gently, 'might I have a word?'

Daphne hesitated, part of her wanting to flee back out into the cold. But Sophie gave her a reassuring nod before discreetly slipping to the side, to chaperone out of earshot. Taking a deep breath, Daphne turned to face Edward.

'I know you have been deeply hurt,' Edward said, his voice low and earnest. 'But I hope in time you can come to trust me. I would never intentionally cause you pain.'

Daphne wavered, old wounds throbbing dully within her breast. Edward's face was open, honest - yet she had been deceived before by seemingly guileless words.

Seeing her doubt, Edward pressed on. 'We cannot change the past. But the future lies unwritten before us. I only ask that you give me a chance to prove myself worthy of your faith.'

He extended his hand, eyes searching hers beseechingly.

Daphne hesitated, tears pricking her eyes. Could she dare open her heart again, make herself so vulnerable? Edward's closeness brought more than just physical heat to her body. She felt drawn to him in a way she had not felt with Lord Alfreton. Slowly, she reached out and placed her hand in Edward's. Though fragile as the falling snow, it was a giant step out of the darkness of her grief.

Sophie watched the tender exchange between Edward and Daphne from across the foyer, her own heart swelling with hope for her sister. Perhaps Edward's persistence would finally break through Daphne's icy reserve.

A shuffling sound beside her made Sophie turn. Nigel had come to stand next to her, hands clasped awkwardly behind his back as he too observed the scene.

'Do you think she will be alright?' Sophie asked softly.

Nigel started a little, as if surprised to be addressed. 'I'm sure Hazelbury will do all he can to help her heal,' he said finally.

Sophie smiled up at him. 'You are a good friend to him. Edward is fortunate to have found someone so devoted.'

Pink spots appeared on Nigel's pale cheeks. He opened his mouth as if to speak, then closed it again, staring down at his shoes.

Sophie felt a pang of sympathy for his shyness. Impulsively, she looped her arm through his. 'Come, let us give them some privacy. I could use some air.'

Sophie indicated to a passing maid that she needed a chaperone.

Nigel let himself be led outside, a look of wonder stealing over his features. As they walked arm in arm into the crisp air, Sophie wondered at the true depth of feeling hidden behind his reticent facade. She only hoped that one day Nigel might find the courage to give voice to it. For now, she would be patient. The seeds of love, once planted, have a way of growing in their own time.

Six

Chapter 6

Daphne stood patiently as Helena fastened the back of her gown - an elegant emerald green silk embroidered with golden flourishes along the hems and neckline. Her customary black gone, she had lost a bet with Sophie the night before in a game of cards. The rich fabric complimented Daphne's dark chestnut hair, which Helena had artfully arranged in cascading curls pinned back on one side with a jade barrette.

'You look absolutely lovely, my lady,' Helena remarked as she helped Daphne into a cashmere overcoat to ward off the winter chill. 'And I know it is not my place to say, but I think His Grace is going to have a hard time looking at anyone else with you dressed like that.'

Daphne offered a small smile of thanks, though her eyes held a glimmer of unease. She dreaded having to make pleasant conversation and pretend all was well in front of the country elite as well as those of London's Ton that were in the vicinity. If only she could avoid Lord Alfreton and his new wife. Word had come that morning that the Alfretons were indeed taking up residence in their country manor for the holidays.

Pushing those gloomy thoughts aside, Daphne joined her family in the awaiting carriage. She gazed out at the snow-cloaked countryside passing by, steeling herself for the afternoon ahead.

The Wintershires' grand estate was already buzzing with activity when the Brookshires arrived. Servers weaved through the clusters of guests proffering trays of lemonade, while a string quartet played a lively Vivaldi concerto.

James quickly became occupied relaying the details of yesterday's hunt with the other gentlemen. Meanwhile, Sophie was whisked into the feminine circles, her pealing laughter rising above the din.

Daphne meandered aimlessly through the rectangular garden, devoid of blooms save evergreen boughs dusted with snow. She nodded politely to familiar faces but largely avoided engaging, feeling disconnected from the frivolity.

'Why the glum face on such a fine winter day?' Edward appeared at her side, looking dashing as ever in his charcoal-tailored coat.

'Simply relishing the tranquillity,' Daphne replied lightly, managing a credibly bright tone.

'Then allow me to accompany you in appreciating this marvellous weather,' Edward offered with a grin. He gestured to a sheltered stone bench beneath a leafless oak tree.

Daphne found herself unexpectedly charmed by his persistence. As they strolled together towards the bench, she realised she had missed their easy rapport these past years. Their conversation soon turned reminiscent, recalling shared childhood misadventures with her brother James. Daphne found herself laughing, Edward's eyes were captivated by her smile.

Just then, a shrill, familiar voice pierced the air. 'Lord and Lady Alfreton, welcome!'

Daphne froze, pulse thrumming. She watched stiffly as the hosts greeted Lord Alfreton and his pretty, blond-haired wife. At the sight of his smile, Daphne's poise wavered, bitterness creeping in. He seemed utterly carefree, with one arm around his wife. Daphne heard a rushing noise in her ears, the world threatened to start spinning. She felt uncomfortably hot, and every muscle in her body screamed at her to run.

Noticing her change in demeanour, Edward followed her gaze. 'Is that...?'

Daphne gave a curt nod unable to speak. Edward's jaw tightened as understanding sank in. 'Would you care to take a turn about the lower garden? It's a bit crowded here. I am sure your sister or brother would accompany us' He offered his arm in polite excuse.

Daphne accepted gratefully, allowing him to guide them away from the merriment. Yet she could not fully relax, her thoughts swirling like the snow flurries around them. Her skin still tingled.

Edward placed a hand over hers. 'He's a fool for letting you go, Daphne. I promise there are those who fully appreciate your worth and always have.' His earnest eyes bore into hers.

Before Daphne could respond, hurried footsteps crunched through the snow behind them.

'Ah, Lady Daphne, what a surprise,' came Lord Alfreton's honeyed voice.

Daphne stiffened, withdrawing her hand from Edward's. She forced a thin smile. 'Lord Alfreton. A pleasure, as always.' She gave a slight nod and made to move away.

'Come now Daphne, no need for such cold formality among old friends,' Alfreton cajoled. 'Let us speak plainly, I have keenly felt your absence in our old circles. Your smile used to light up the room. That brooch is new, is it not?' Alfreton indicated to the brooch clipped in the centre of Daphne's bodice. 'The ruby reminds me of a ring you once wore. I often think back to when I first saw it adorning your graceful hand.'

'Lord Alfreton, I do not believe we have cause to speak plainly to one another. You broke our acquaintance and I have no desire to reestablish it.' Daphne felt joy surging through her. Her anxiety began to fade away as she realised the man before her was trying to manipulate her. She straightened her spine, she would not allow him to have any further hold over her. 'Good day Lord Alfreton.'

'Daphne, wait' Lord Alfreton raised a hand to grab Daphne's arm.

Edward stepped forward, blue eyes blazing. 'I believe *Lady* Daphne made her sentiments clear. It would be best if you take your leave.'

Alfreton glared incredulously. 'And who are you to make such a demand?'

'The Duke of Hazelbury. And one not inclined to allow further distress to

Lady Daphne.' Edward kept his voice low but firm with restrained fury.

Sensing imminent scandal, Alfreton forced a tight laugh. 'Very well. Daphne, a pleasure as always.' He offered a mocking bow before departing.

Daphne released a quivering breath. 'Thank you,' she said softly, gratitude welling within her heart. She realised her hands were shaking.

'Here, sit on this bench a moment and compose yourself.' Edward led Daphne to a small bench slightly out of view of the main party. He too needed a moment to compose himself. The nerve of Alfreton, acting as though he was still a suitor for Daphne, dropping her title when speaking to her. He noticed his hands were shaking almost as much as Daphne's. He crouched down to look Daphne in the eyes. 'I do not like that man. I am glad that he ended his courtship of you. You are worth far more than that.' He took her hand in his, rubbing his thumb over the back of it.

'I will be fine in a moment I am sure' Daphne stared at their joined hands. Heat flooded through her. Alfreton's appearance had flustered her, his words had angered her. Edward's words had soothed her, his hand now grounding her. She felt an overwhelming urge to throw her arms around him and cry. Seeing Alfreton and Edward together released all her thoughts of Alfreton. He had broken her heart, but somewhere along the way it had mended, and Daphne was afraid she may have already given it to Edward.

'Daphne! Are you out here?' James' voice floated from the other side of the hedge she was sitting against. Rounding the corner, James became concerned when he saw Daphne sitting on the bench. 'Daphne, are you alright? Sophie saw you talking to Alfreton and was worried.'

'I am fine. Edward was my knight in shining armour and sent him away.' Tears threatened to fall from her eyes. 'Seeing him has shaken me a little, however, it has made me realise Alfreton was not the one for me. I am going to take back Christmas.'

'Come.' Edward pulled Daphne to her feet. 'Let us get you some lemonade. I am sure if we get you at a table with James, Sophie, Thistleton and myself you will feel much better. Show of force and all.'

By the time their carriage rolled to a stop outside Brookshire Manor, Daphne felt a peace she had not felt for a long time. Her siblings had noticed the change in her.

Seven

Chapter 7

The sun glittered brightly off the freshly fallen snow as the Brookshire carriage rolled up the long drive to Jasper Park. Daphne gazed out of the frost-lined window, admiring the snow-covered fir trees flanking the road. She inhaled deeply, the crisp winter air mingling with hints of wood-smoke and roasting meat emanating from the manor ahead.

'It was so kind of Edward to invite us,' Sophie remarked from her seat opposite Daphne. 'And on Christmas Eve too!'

'Yes, how thoughtful,' Daphne replied quietly, a mix of anticipation and unease welling within her. She smoothed her emerald velvet gown, secretly hoping to make a good impression on Edward today.

Beside Sophie, her brother James leaned back into the plush leather, seemingly oblivious to the sisters' conversation. 'At least Hazelbury keeps an excellent table,' he commented. 'One grows so tired of hare and venison this time of year.'

Sophie shot him a reproachful look while Daphne suppressed a grin. Trust her brother to focus on the menu ahead of their company.

As the carriage rolled to a stop before the imposing double doors, liveried footmen hurried forth to unfold the steps. James stepped down first, then turned to assist Sophie. Daphne gathered her skirts, accepting James' outstretched hand. Her kidskin boots crunched on the gravel drive.

The massive doors opened, and there stood Edward silhouetted against the grand foyer, a very fine image of the Lord of the Manor.

'Welcome, my friends,' he greeted them warmly, eyes crinkling with undisguised delight.

Daphne's pulse quickened as Edward's gaze met hers. 'Thank you for having us, your Grace,' she managed steadily, dropping into a curtsy.

Edward bowed in return. 'The pleasure is all mine. Please, come in from the cold.' He ushered them into the vaulted entrance hall where a crackling fire already blazed in the hearth, warming the room against the winter chill outside. Garlands of pine and holly adorned the banisters, infusing the air with notes of festive greenery.

'You have lovely decorations, your Grace,' Sophie remarked as the butler relieved her of her cloak.

'I can't take much credit I'm afraid. Mrs. Pemberton is the genius behind it all.' Edward's eyes twinkled at their pretend formality.

As if on cue, an elderly woman emerged from a side passage, her keen eyes alighting on the new arrivals.

'Ah, our guests have arrived! Welcome, welcome!' She clasped her hands in delight. 'Come now, let's get you all some hot mulled cider and roast chestnuts to take off the cold.'

'That sounds divine,' laughed Sophie. 'Lead the way!'

Linking her arm through James', Sophie followed the housekeeper towards the parlour where drinks and Nigel awaited.

The grand parlour of Jasper Park was aglow with the warm light of a hundred candles. Garlands of holly and pine adorned the mantle, filling the air with the fresh scent of the forest. The focal point of the room was the fireplace, its mantle laden with shimmering ornaments, silver tinsel, and pops of tartan ribbon.

'It's beautiful, is it not?' said Edward, joining Daphne beside the crackling fire. 'I know Christmas may not hold the fondest memories for you, but I was rather hoping to make some new ones this year.'

Daphne gazed around the room, the flickering candles casting a soft glow across her face. 'It has been far too long since I've celebrated properly.'

'Which is why,' said Edward, rubbing his hands together, 'I have planned a little scavenger hunt for this afternoon. I have hidden clues all about the estate that will lead you to various locations, each with a surprise gift waiting.'

Daphne tilted her head. 'All this for me?'

'I want you to rediscover the joy of Christmas, Daphne. To replace old wounds with new memories.' Edward's eyes crinkled warmly. 'Will you join me?'

Daphne hesitated, memories of past grief flickering through her mind. Yet gazing at Edward's earnest expression, she felt a glimmer of something she'd thought long lost hope.

'Very well,' she said at last. 'I accept your challenge, sir.'

Edward grinned. 'Excellent. I promise you will not regret it.'

'Oh, look! Is that a small fir tree?' Sophie called out as she spotted the six-foot tree in the corner of the room.

'Yes,' Nigel's eyes lit up. 'Hazelbury is being kind to me in pandering to my home's traditions. I do hope you will all help me decorate it this afternoon.' His awkwardness seemed to evaporate.

'Well, I surely will.' Sophie almost bounced at the idea of getting to decorate the tree. 'I am positive we can get James to help with the higher branches.'

James looked up, an almond from the nut bowl halfway to his mouth. 'Why not! Maybe a new tradition is what Daphne needs to start enjoying Christmas again.'

Daphne observed her younger sister's cheer with bittersweet fondness. Sophie had always loved Christmas.

The dining room at Jasper Park was intimate but elegant, with a gleaming mahogany table surrounded by upholstered chairs. A sideboard held an array of savoury dishes: slices of honey-glazed ham, wedges of creamy brie, fresh grapes and figs, and fluffy dinner rolls still steaming from the oven.

Edward held out a chair for Daphne. She smoothed her skirts and sat, intensely aware of his lingering touch on her shoulder. Sophie, Nigel and James took their seats while servants bustled about, pouring wine and filling plates with delicacies.

'Everything looks wonderful, your Grace,' Sophie said, leaning over to inhale the aroma of the steaming rolls.

'Mrs. Pemberton outdid herself, as always,' Edward replied, settling into his chair at the head of the table. He turned to Daphne. 'I hope you find it agreeable?'

Daphne nodded. 'Of course. You are too kind to host us all today.' She hoped her voice did not reveal the butterflies still fluttering inside after his earlier revelation.

Plates full, the quintet fell into easy conversation, remarking on the uncommonly clear weather and plans for the Christmas holiday. Daphne stayed quiet for the most part, distracted by the feeling of Edward's leg occasionally brushing hers beneath the table.

James dove into the spread ravenously. 'My compliments to the cook,' he declared between bites of ham. 'The winter air seems to have given me a fierce appetite!'

Sophie gave him a reproachful look, but Edward just chuckled. 'I'm pleased to see you enjoying it. Eat your fill, there's plenty more.'

Sunlight streamed through the mullioned windows as the meal continued, warming Daphne from within and without. She savoured a sip of wine, feeling a sense of peace and belonging that had eluded her for so long. This Christmas Eve lunch was shaping up to be one of the merriest in recent memory.

Daphne started to feel the beginnings of contentment as they moved back to the parlour. Her anxieties and fears over the Christmas period began to slip away as she enjoyed her time with her family and friends.

'Daphne!' Sophie paused her investigation of the tree to wave eagerly. 'Come see what Edward has planned!' With a small smile, Daphne joined Sophie by the 'grand' fir. 'Can you believe it?' Sophie grasped Daphne's hands, eyes shining. 'A Christmas scavenger hunt! Oh, it shall be such fun for you. James and Lord Thistleson have agreed to go skating on the pond with me.'

Daphne nodded, though her chest tightened. 'Yes, quite thrilling,' she managed.

49

Sophie tipped her head, brows furrowing. 'You seem hesitant, dear sister. I know Christmas brings some sad memories for you, but will you not give Edward's surprise a chance?'

Daphne sighed, gazing into Sophie's hopeful face. Perhaps she could try, for her sister's sake, to release the lingering grief of Christmases past. She felt almost reluctant to give up that last vestige of fear. 'You are right, Sophie,' she conceded. 'I… I shall do my best.'

'Wonderful!' Sophie squeezed Daphne's hands. 'Now come, we must not keep the gentlemen waiting!' Linking arms, the two sisters stepped out into the crisp winter air. The scavenger hunt was about to begin.

Edward stood on the grand front steps, looking dashing in his tailcoat and top hat. Beside him waited the gangly, ginger-haired Nigel, fidgeting with his gloves whilst shooting glances at James who was casually lounging against the step's bannister.

Edward smiled warmly as Sophie and Daphne approached. 'I trust you are prepared for a Christmas adventure?' He offered Daphne a leather-bound journal and quill. 'This shall help document your quest. And here is the first clue.'

With a flourish, he presented an envelope sealed in red wax. Daphne accepted it hesitantly, her guarded gaze meeting his.

'Go on,' he encouraged. 'Let the hunt commence!'

Sliding her fingernail beneath the wax, Daphne unfolded the heavy parchment inside. Sophie leaned in eagerly as Daphne read aloud:

'Beneath branches of green, a gift can be seen. Look for the angel who marks where it has been.'

'The garden maze!' Sophie exclaimed. 'Come, Lord Thistleson, we must hurry! Maybe we will get Edward's prize if we beat Daphne.' Laughing gaily, she seized Nigel's arm and whisked him down the garden path, his lanky form stumbling to match her pace. James wondered after them, cradling a basket of goodies Mrs. Pemberton had prepared him to keep him going throughout the afternoon.

Daphne watched them go, her eyes sad. 'Must we participate in these silly games?' she asked Edward.

He stepped closer, voice gentle. 'Humour me, Daphne. You may find it reminds you of happier times.'

With a resigned sigh, she nodded. 'Lead the way then.'

Together they strolled towards the garden, the sound of Sophie calling out to James floating back to them on the air.

Daphne followed Edward down the winding garden paths, frost crunching underfoot. The hedges loomed tall on either side, decorated with ribbons and pinecones. Up ahead, she could hear Sophie's voice raised in delight, likely upon discovering the next clue.

Daphne paused, closing her eyes. She inhaled deeply, the sharp scent of evergreen mingling with wood-smoke. It reminded her of childhood days spent frolicking outside, building snowmen and sipping hot cider by the fireside after. A faint smile touched her lips.

'What is it?' Edward asked gently.

'Nothing…just a memory.' Daphne opened her eyes. 'Shall we continue?'

They rounded a corner and she gasped. Ahead, an angel statue stood in an alcove, one hand extended in offering. Dangling from her fingers was a small gift box wrapped in gold paper. Daphne lifted it carefully, giving the angel a grateful pat. Untying the ribbon, she revealed a cameo brooch inside.

'It was my mother's,' Edward said softly. 'I thought you might wish to wear it today.'

She swallowed hard. 'Help me put it on?' He obliged, fingers brushing her collarbone as he fastened the pin. Daphne shivered, pulse quickening. 'Thank you,' she whispered. Taking up her journal, she penned a description of the clue's solution. A new energy quickened her steps as they ventured deeper into the maze, the spirit of Christmas awakening in her heart.

Daphne and Edward continued through the hedge maze, the cold air nipping at their cheeks. Up ahead, they heard Sophie's melodic laughter mingling with Nigel's deeper chuckles.

Daphne paused, tilting her head. 'They seem to be getting on well,' she remarked.

Edward smiled knowingly. 'Thistleson is quite taken with your sister. I believe he wishes to declare himself, if he can summon the courage.'

'Truly?' Daphne's eyes widened. She had noticed Sophie's blushes around the bashful Nigel but had not realised the depth of his affection.

'Indeed. He confided in me just this morning.' Edward leaned closer, his breath ticking her cheek. 'I suspect before long we shall be celebrating another happy union.'

Daphne's heart quickened at his nearness and the intimation in his words. Clearing her throat, she gestured down the path. 'Shall we catch up to them?'

As they rounded the corner, Sophie and Nigel came into view beside the frozen pond, James sat nearby continuing to investigate his basket. Nigel was attempting to guide Sophie in a waltz on the ice, both laughing gaily when they slipped. Skates lay nearby, Edward had thought of everything.

Daphne's breath caught at the tender scene. For a moment, she saw herself and Edward reflected in the younger couple - carefree, in love, embracing the magic of the season.

Taking Edward's arm, she stepped back, allowing Nigel and Sophie their privacy. Perhaps she had been too quick to dismiss the gifts of Christmas this year. With Edward and Sophie beside her, there was still light and hope to be found. Edward excused himself to prepare her "prize" for finishing the hunt and left her to continue.

* * *

Nigel glided slowly across the frozen pond; one hand tucked behind his back while the other held Sophie's mittened hand gently as they skated. Though his skating was sure and steady, his palms were slick with nervous sweat inside his wool gloves.

He darted a glance at Sophie's rosy, smiling face as she hummed a carol, her blonde curls peeking out from under her scarlet bonnet. His heart swelled and he swallowed hard, gathering his courage.

'Sophie, I... I have something I must tell you,' he stammered.

Sophie stopped humming and turned her bright blue eyes on him. 'Yes, my lord?'

He gulped, bringing them both to a stop. 'We have spent much time together these past weeks and I have felt myself growing…quite fond of you.' Sophie's eyes widened. Nigel's face flushed crimson but he pressed on. 'In truth, from the moment I first saw you, I was taken with your warmth and beauty.' He fished in his pocket and extracted a small parcel. 'I know it is forward of me, but I wondered if you might accept this small token of my esteem?'

Sophie accepted the gift with trembling fingers. As she unwrapped a silver brooch shaped like a robin, tears of joy sprung to her eyes.

'Oh, Nigel!' she cried. 'I have grown so very fond of you too!' At her words, Nigel's face broke into a radiant smile. Taking her hands in his, the two gazed at each other, hearts brimming with emotion. The ice and chill were forgotten; in that moment, it was only the two of them.

Caught up in the tender moment, Nigel gently pulled Sophie closer. She lifted her face to his, eyes shining. Their breaths mingled in icy puffs as he leaned down and captured her lips in a soft, tentative kiss.

Sophie's eyes fluttered closed as she returned the kiss. Nigel's arms encircled Sophie's waist as she wrapped hers around his neck. The kiss deepened, warming them against the winter chill.

When at last they drew apart, Sophie rested her head against Nigel's chest with a contented sigh. His heart thudded beneath her ear.

'I saw that Thistleson!' James' voice floated across the ice. 'You had better be ready to talk to my father.' Sophie lifted her head to glare at her brother before putting it back.

They held each other close as snowflakes drifted down around them. The ice glimmered under the winter sunlight. In that magical moment between them, the true spirit of Christmas was rekindled.

* * *

The crunch of Daphne's boots punctured the silence as she hurried along the snow-dusted garden path, her breath forming frosty plumes in the icy air. Her pulse quickened as she followed the trail of cryptic clues leading her deeper into the shadowed grounds of the estate. Though initially reluctant, she soon found herself caught up in the exhilaration of Edward's elaborate scavenger hunt. At each secluded spot, she uncovered a puzzle or riddle tucked away that sent her darting off in search of the next hidden surprise, skirts swishing through the drifts. With growing enthusiasm, she scoured behind every snow-laden bush, gazed up into the barren boughs of every towering oak, and peered behind ice-encrusted statues. The bitter cold could not touch her now, not with the thrill of discovery lighting a glow within. She eagerly traced Edward's meticulous steps through the silvery landscape, marvelling at the care and tenderness he had taken in planning it all for her.

At a secluded gazebo draped in pine garlands and red ribbons, she found a tiny package tucked away. Hands trembling, she unwrapped it to reveal a silver locket engraved with her initials. Inside was a portrait of her and Edward as children.

Tears pricked Daphne's eyes as memories flooded back. Laughter on Christmas mornings, building snowmen in the gardens, sharing stolen sweetmeats on the stairs. Her bitterness towards the holiday had made her forget so much joy.

Slipping the locket over her neck, she pressed on with renewed vigour. The final clue was hidden here somewhere, she just knew it. As the scavenger hunt neared its conclusion, her heart swelled with anticipation. This Christmas would not be marked by heartbreak and loss. Not this time. Edward had reminded her of the hope the season could bring. She was ready now to let the light back in.

At last, Daphne found the final clue hidden in a nook beneath a rose bush. With shaking fingers, she unfolded the parchment to reveal a delicate script. It read:

'Follow the path of my delight,

To where the tree stands tall and bright.

There you'll find the greatest gift,

One that will lift your heart and soul to lift.'

Turning in confusion of 'my delight', Daphne saw a path leading away lined with the shrub, 'Daphne'. Smiling to herself she followed it, the snow crunching softly under her boots. As she turned the final corner, she gasped at the sight that greeted her.

A towering evergreen tree stood in the centre of a clearing, its branches dripping with sparkling ornaments and shimmering tinsel. Beneath it, a blanket of snow had been cleared away to reveal a patch of soft grass. The air was filled with the scent of pine and cinnamon.

As she approached the tree, Edward stepped out from behind it, a wide smile on his face. 'Merry Christmas,' he said, taking her hand. 'I hope you enjoyed the scavenger hunt. Do you like the tree?' He pointed at the ornaments. 'Thistleson helped me, it is what he grew up with, I thought you would like the spectacle'.

Daphne's heart swelled with gratitude and joy as she gazed up at Edward. 'It was wonderful,' she said, her voice choked with emotion. 'Thank you for reminding me of the magic of Christmas.'

Edward's eyes shone with affection as he pulled her closer, wrapping an arm around her. 'There is one more surprise,' he said, gesturing towards the tree.

Daphne's eyes widened as she saw a small box sitting beneath the boughs. Edward knelt down and retrieved it, holding it out to her. 'Open it,' he said, his voice gentle and tender.

Daphne's fingers trembled as she lifted the lid. Inside was a delicate diamond ring, its silver band glinting in the sunlight. She gasped, tears springing to her eyes. 'Edward, it is beautiful,' she said, her voice barely above a whisper.

Edward took the ring from the box and slipped it onto Daphne's finger. 'It's a promise,' he said, his voice low and earnest. 'A promise that we will face whatever life throws our way, together.'

Daphne threw her arms around Edward's neck, holding him tight. 'Thank you,' she whispered. 'I never want to forget the magic of this moment.'

Edward held her close, his heart full of love and contentment. The snow continued to fall around them, but they were lost in their own world of warmth and happiness. In that moment, they knew that nothing could ever take this moment away from them. The magic of Christmas had brought them together, and they knew that they would never let it go.

Eight

Chapter 8

❦

The grand foyer of Brookshire Manor glowed with the warm light of beeswax candles. Crimson ribbons and holly sprigs adorned the banisters while the scent of cinnamon and cloves perfumed the air. Sophie hummed "God Rest Ye Merry Gentlemen" as she tied another velvet bow atop the garland wrapped around the staircase. Her golden curls bounced with each step while her cheeks bloomed a rosy pink.

'Oh, what fun the holidays have brought this year!' she exclaimed to no one in particular.

The heavy oak doors groaned open, ushering in a swirl of snowflakes and two very cold gentlemen. Sophie skipped down the stairs to greet them.

'Lord Hazelbury, Lord Thistleson, welcome!'

Nigel offered a shy half-smile in reply while Edward bowed theatrically.

'We apologise for the intrusion, Lady Sophie,' said Edward. 'Your father was kind enough to invite us to join your family for Christmas mass.'

Sophie beamed. 'The more the merrier! Please warm yourselves by the fire while I fetch Father.' The butler, Thomas, removed their coats and led them into the parlour.

She scurried off, leaving the men to shake off the chill. Nigel held his chilled

56

fingers toward the hearth, too cold to initiate conversation. Edward filled the silence.

'I am eager to see how Daphne fares today.' He stared pensively into the flickering flames. 'I am hoping our afternoon yesterday broke her from her melancholy. She did seem happier when we decorated the tree after the scavenger hunt and your ice skating.'

Nigel nodded. 'One can only hope, though a broken heart takes time to heal.'

At that moment, Lord Brookshire's voice boomed through the hall. 'Gentlemen, so glad you could join us!'

Sophie peeked around the corner, watching Nigel jump at her father's sudden entrance. She stifled a giggle. Drawing the shy ginger out of his shell would be her Christmas challenge this year.

The morning sun glinted off the fresh blanket of snow as Daphne and Edward strolled arm-in-arm through the estate's gardens, the poor maid, Helena, trailing after, blowing on her hands trying to warm her fingertips. Daphne tilted her face skyward, eyes closed as she breathed in the crisp, cold air.

'I had nearly forgotten how lovely the gardens look in winter,' she remarked. 'The barren trees make one appreciate the simple elegance of the land itself.'

Edward gazed at her fondly. 'As this winter makes one appreciate the warmth of spring to come.' Daphne managed a small smile, knowing he referred to her heartbreak gradually thawing after her two years.

They walked in comfortable silence for a time, boots crunching on the snowy path. Daphne paused by the frozen fountain.

'I used to love tossing coins and making wishes here as a child,' she mused.

Edward paused, then drew a small velvet box from his coat pocket. 'Perhaps you'd make one more?'

Daphne's eyes widened as he opened the box, revealing an intricate silver bracelet dotted with sapphires.

'Oh Edward…' She gingerly lifted the bracelet from the box, tears glistening. 'It is absolutely exquisite. However did you…'

'I saw it in London on the way through and thought of your eyes, little did

I know then that I would fall in love with those eyes again.' he said softly. He gently clasped it around her wrist. 'Consider it a Christmas gift. To new beginnings.'

Daphne thanked him, heart swelling. He loved her. Perhaps she would find joy again after all.

Daphne dabbed at her eyes, overcome with emotion. Edward tucked her arm in his and together they meandered back towards the manor.

As they entered the parlour, the smell of cooking welcomed them. Sophie was on a step stool hanging a garland over the mantle, humming "God Rest Ye Merry Gentlemen" again. Daphne thought that she really must teach Sophie some new songs, or maybe get Nigel to teach her some from the continent.

She turned, nearly toppling from her perch. 'Daphne! Edward!'

Sophie hopped down, clasping Daphne's hands excitedly. 'Oh, your bracelet, how exquisite!' Then in a conspiratorial whisper, 'I do think Edward means to make his intentions known!'

Daphne flushed. 'Perhaps, in time.'

Just then, Lady Brookshire entered, followed by Nigel, James and Lord Brookshire. 'Darlings, you've returned just in time for wassail.'

The family gathered round the hearth as a servant began ladling the hot cider. Nigel stood awkwardly to the side until Sophie took his arm.

'Come my lord, you simply must try Cook's wassail.' She smiled encouragingly and Nigel managed a shy grin in return.

As they sipped, Lady Brookshire said fondly, 'Remember when we'd act out the nativity after church? Sophie always wanted to play Mary.'

'James made a very wise Joseph,' Lord Brookshire chuckled.

Daphne gazed at the hearth, memories washing over her. Perhaps she had shut out too much joy these past months. She joined in the reminiscences, treasuring each moment. For the first time in long while, her heart felt full of Christmas once more.

Sophie set down her cup, eyes sparkling. 'I almost forgot! Nigel, this is for you.' She presented him with a small box.

Nigel reddened. 'For me?' He took it gingerly and untied the bow. Nestled inside was a golden pocket watch, engraved with his initials.

'Sophie...' Nigel looked up, at a loss for words.

'Turn it over,' Sophie said softly.

On the back was inscribed: "To Nigel, with affection. Joyeux Noël".

'It's perfect.' Nigel fastened the watch to his waistcoat. 'I don't know how to thank you.'

'Seeing your smile is thanks enough.' Sophie squeezed his hand.

Nigel met her gaze. 'You've made this Christmas truly special. My time here with you and your family has been a gift.'

Lord Brookshire clapped Nigel on the back. 'We are pleased you could join us. Any friend of Edward's is most welcome.'

Lady Brookshire dabbed her eyes with a handkerchief, emotional in the belief that it was her matchmaking skills that had brought Sophie and Nigel together. 'Oh, do look at the time. We must be off to church.'

As they prepared to depart, Daphne felt her heart swelling with gratitude. This Christmas had proven more magical than she could have imagined. With Edward and her family beside her, she looked forward to greeting the new year with hope and joy.

Nigel lingered behind as the others headed outside, fidgeting with his cuffs.

'Is something wrong?' Sophie asked gently.

'No, not at all.' Nigel took a deep breath. 'I just wanted to give you one more gift before we leave.'

He pulled a small box from his pocket and presented it to Sophie with trembling hands. She looked at him quizzically before opening it. Inside was a posy ring, engraved on the inside with "God rest ye merry gentlemen".

Sophie's eyes widened in surprise. She looked back and forth between the ring and Nigel's expectant face.

'My lord, I... this is...' Sophie stammered.

Before she could finish, Nigel suddenly dropped to one knee, taking Sophie's hands in her own.

'Sophie Brookshire, you are the kindest, gentlest woman I have ever known,' he began, voice thick with emotion. 'This Christmas, you have made me happier than I ever dreamed. I know this may seem sudden, but I am certain of my feelings.' He paused, gathering courage. 'Sophie, I love you with all my heart. Will you make me the happiest man in England and the continent by consenting to be my wife?'

Sophie gaped in astonishment, at a complete loss for words. After a moment, a radiant smile spread across her face.

'Oh Nigel, my darling Nigel,' she breathed, pulling him up into an embrace. 'Nothing could make me happier than to be your wife. If you will have me, I am yours forever.' Sophie let out a joyous laugh, throwing her arms around Nigel's neck. Tears of happiness shone in her eyes. 'Of course I will have you!' She exclaimed. 'This is the best Christmas gift I could have ever imagined.'

Their lips met in a tender kiss, full of promise for their future ahead. Arm in arm, they walked out into the softly falling snow, their hearts overflowing with love.

After church, the family gathered in the parlour, abuzz with excitement over the newly announced engagement.

'Congratulations, my dears!' Lady Brookshire exclaimed, embracing Sophie and Nigel in turn. 'We are so happy for you both.'

James shook Nigel's hand firmly, his eyes crinkling with delight. 'Welcome to the family. I know you will make Sophie very happy.'

Daphne hugged her sister, tears of joy glistening on her cheeks. 'Oh Sophie, I am so thrilled for you! And my lord, you must know you are gaining the most wonderful sister.'

Sophie beamed, leaning into Nigel's side. His arm wrapped securely around her waist, as if he never planned to let go.

Edward clapped Nigel on the back. 'Excellent work, old chap! I daresay you have outdone us all with this surprise.' He winked at Daphne, who blushed prettily.

The family gathered around the piano and sang hymns, their voices ringing through the manor. Cook bustled in with a tray of hot cider, her round face wreathed in smiles for the newly betrothed couple.

As the last notes of "God Rest Ye Merry Gentlemen" faded, Lord Brookshire raised his glass. 'To Nigel and Sophie, and their future happiness together.'

'Here, here!' everyone chorused, toasting the beaming pair.

Nigel ducked his head shyly, then met Sophie's loving gaze. In that moment, with their family surrounding them, the promise of Christmas felt truly magical.

Daphne sighed contentedly. After the pain and heartbreak, she had endured, it felt good to revel in pure joy again. As carols floated on the air and laughter pealed, she found herself smiling, her gloom dissipating.

Perhaps she had allowed her wounds to linger too long, casting a shadow over the present. Seeing Sophie's radiant happiness reminded Daphne that light still existed in the world, even after loss.

Daphne gazed around at the people she loved, their faces glowing in the firelight. She inhaled the scent of cinnamon and pine, listening to the crackle of logs. This was Christmas as she remembered - cozy and magical. For the first time in years, contentment washed over her. The house brimmed with warmth and merriment, chasing away the winter chill.

As snow drifted past the frost-laced windows, Daphne let the final shards of grief fall away. Here, surrounded by family, she had found her way home. Joy and light-filled her heart once more.

Sitting next to Edward on the settee, she lent in close to ask a question. 'I assume my father already knows as he has approved this match. But I fear I do not know Lord Thistleson's standing in society. Just that he is your friend and a Lord.'

'That he is my friend is not enough?' Edward gave a sly smile. 'His father is an Earl up around the Lake District. He does not come to town. His mother had ties to the House of Wettin and other prominent families on the continent.'

Daphne's eyes went wide. 'But... Thistleson...' Daphne could not believe what Edward was saying, Nigel seemed so awkward with himself that seemed at odds with the thought that he might be related to royalty. Edward laughed at Daphne's confusion.

Nine

Chapter 9

❧~❀~❧

Brookshire Manor glowed with the warm light of a hundred candles. Garlands of holly and pine adorned the banisters, their glossy leaves twinkling with shards of tinsel. The banister in the foyer dripped with crystals and gold ribbon, casting flickering shadows across the polished floors.

Daphne stood beneath the mistletoe hung above the doorway, her fingers worrying the silk sash of her gown. She watched the dancing flames in the hearth, lost in thought, until a footstep sounded behind her. She turned to find Edward gazing at her, his eyes bright beneath furrowed brows.

'Good evening,' he said softly.

Daphne's lips curved in a timid smile. 'Good evening.'

Edward moved closer, the firelight playing over his face. 'Forgive my boldness, but you look lovely tonight.'

A blush rose on Daphne's cheeks. She lowered her gaze. 'You are too kind.'

'I only speak the truth.' Edward paused and rubbed his palms along his trousers. 'Might I have the honour of your company for a stroll outside?' He indicated to a maid to have a chaperone acquired.

Daphne nodded, breath quickening as Edward offered his arm. She took it lightly, pulse racing at his nearness. They both wrapped themselves in coats.

Together they passed beneath the mistletoe's white berries and out into the crisp, silent night.

Edward led Daphne along the snow-dusted path that wound through the gardens behind the manor. Moonlight filtered through the bare tree branches, casting a silver glow over the frozen landscape. Daphne shivered and drew her fur-lined coat tighter around her shoulders.

'Are you cold?' Edward asked, concern furrowing his brow. 'We can go back inside.'

'No,' Daphne assured him. 'The fresh air is lovely.' They walked on in silence for a few moments until they reached the stone fountain at the garden's centre. Edward guided Daphne to sit beside him on the fountain's edge. He took her delicate hands in his own.

'Daphne,' he began, 'from the moment I arrived, I felt something between us I cannot explain. In your eyes, I sense a kindred spirit, one who understands the deeper longings of the heart.'

Daphne's breath caught, pulse racing. She met his earnest gaze.

'Forgive my presumption,' Edward continued, 'but I must speak my feelings, even if they are not returned. Daphne, you are unlike any woman I have known. Your beauty, your grace, your tenderness…you have captured my heart completely.'

He paused, searching her face. Daphne's eyes glistened with emotion. With sincerity resonating in each word, Edward said, 'Daphne Brookshire, would you do me the honour of becoming my wife?'

Daphne's voice trembled. 'Edward, I thought love lost to me forever. But you have shown me hope still lives in the heart. Yes, I will marry you.'

Joy lit Edward's face. He drew Daphne into his embrace beneath the moonlight as silent snowflakes began to fall.

Daphne could scarcely believe the words she had just uttered. Mere weeks ago, her heart had been shrouded in grief, convinced no light would pierce its darkness again. Yet here, encircled in Edward's arms, the first tender blossoms of new love unfurled within her.

Daphne gazed up at her beloved through tear-filled eyes. 'My dearest Edward,' she whispered. 'You have given me such happiness this night, I can scarce contain it.'

Just then, the sound of cheering and applause broke the stillness. Daphne and Edward turned to see James, Sophie and Nigel gathered at the garden's edge, joyful witnesses to their felicity.

Sophie rushed forward, throwing her arms around her sister. 'Oh Daphne, I am so happy for you!' she exclaimed. Dabbing her eyes with a handkerchief, she added, 'I just knew this Christmas would bring you joy again.'

Nigel approached as well, extending a hand to Edward. 'Congratulations, my friend,' he said with a rare smile. 'May your future together be blessed.'

James gave Daphne a hug. 'Sorry for intruding on the moment, but Edward gave us a warning of his intentions and Sophie refused to stay inside.'

'You were just as eager as I was to get out here.' Sophie poked their brother in the side.

As Daphne gazed at the smiling faces surrounding them, her heart swelled with gratitude. This was a Christmas she would cherish forever.

Ten

Epilogue

One year later...

Brookshire estate was alive with the sounds of laughter and merriment. Garlands of holly and evergreen adorned the banisters, their scent mingling with the aromas of wassail and figgy pudding.

Daphne glided through the room, her cheeks flushed and eyes bright. On her finger glittered the diamond ring, sparkling in the candlelight. At her side was Edward, as handsome as ever, his arm wrapped around her waist.

'Happy Christmas, my love,' he murmured, pressing a kiss to her temple.

'The happiest,' Daphne replied, leaning into him contentedly.

Across the hall, Sophie whirled across the dance floor in Nigel's arms, her golden curls bouncing. Though once bashful, Nigel now gazed at his bride with unconcealed adoration.

Daphne's heart swelled at the sight. How much had changed in a year! Last Christmas she had been mired in grief, never dreaming she could find love again. Yet here they were - two sisters reunited with their hearts healed. As Edward drew her close once more, Daphne offered up a silent prayer of thanks. Out of sorrow, joy had bloomed at last.

Daphne's reverie was interrupted by a cheerful voice calling her name. She turned to see her mother bustling towards them, face flushed from the heat of the hearths.

'Oh, my dears, I'm so delighted you could join us this year!' Lady Brookshire exclaimed, embracing them warmly. 'Just look at how perfectly everything has come together.'

She gestured around the hall, which was truly a sight to behold. Garlands of holly lined the walls while mistletoe dangled above each doorway. A towering fir tree stood in the corner, a nod to Nigel's childhood, adorned with candles and colourful baubles that glimmered in the firelight.

'You have outdone yourself, Mother,' Daphne said sincerely. Though Christmas decor had once brought her pain, she now felt only joy at the beautiful scene before her.

'I must admit, it is rather magical,' Lady Brookshire replied with a twinkle in her eye. 'But it's not the trimmings that make a home at Christmas - it's having all my loved ones together under one roof.'

Daphne slipped an arm around her mother's shoulders. 'How right you are,' she said softly.

As music played merrily on the pianoforte, the two generations stood together surveying the festivities. Laughter rang out as Sophie and Nigel danced past, while Edward chatted amiably with Daphne's father by the fire.

Daphne's heart swelled once more. Truly, this was everything she had ever hoped Christmas could be - a time of joy, light, and family.

'Happy Christmas, Mama,' she whispered.

'The happiest, my dear,' Lady Brookshire replied, squeezing her daughter close. 'The very happiest.'

Sophie and Nigel whirled across the dance floor, lost in their own little world. Though the steps came easily to Sophie, Nigel moved awkwardly, his eyes glued to his feet. Yet whenever he glanced up at his new bride, his face transformed with a besotted smile.

As the music swelled, Sophie playfully spun Nigel out before drawing him back into her arms. Caught off guard, he stumbled into her embrace. Sophie let out a silvery laugh and Nigel's cheeks flushed pink, though his eyes shone with adoration.

'You're a natural, Lord Thistleson,' Sophie teased.

'Only because I have the perfect partner,' Nigel replied earnestly.

Sophie's grin softened into an affectionate smile. Reaching up, she gently brushed an unruly lock of hair from Nigel's forehead. He leaned into her touch, the simple gesture speaking volumes.

Around the smitten newlyweds, the atmosphere buzzed with Christmas cheer. Lady Brookshire chatted animatedly with the cook about the evening's feast while Lord Brookshire entertained guests with amusing tales from his youth.

Carollers gathered around the piano; their voices raised in joyful chorus.

As she watched her friends and family revel in the spirit of the season, Daphne's heart swelled with gratitude. The pain that had once clouded her Christmas joy had melted away, leaving only light and hope for the future.

Daphne slipped away from the merriment, seeking a moment of solitude. She wandered into the library, its dark oak shelves and plush Persian rug offering a hushed respite. A fire crackled low in the hearth, casting flickering shadows over the room.

She moved to the window and gazed out at the moonlit grounds blanketed in new fallen snow. The peaceful scene soothed her soul. A pair of strong arms encircled her waist. Daphne leaned back against Edward's broad chest with a contented sigh. For a long moment, neither spoke, simply savouring the quiet intimacy.

'What are you thinking about, my love?' Edward murmured.

'How much my life has changed this past year,' Daphne replied. 'I never imagined I could feel such joy, especially at Christmas. You have given me so much happiness.'

She turned in his arms to face him. The firelight danced in Edward's eyes as he gazed at her, his expression tender.

'This time last year, I had all but given up hope of ever finding love,' Daphne confessed. 'But you saw through my loneliness and brought light back into my dreary world.'

Reaching up, she cradled Edward's cheek in her palm. 'I will be forever grateful that you came back into my life. You are the greatest gift I could ever receive.'

Overcome with emotion, Edward drew her close and kissed her deeply. Daphne melted into his embrace, her heart overflowing.

As they parted, Edward rested his forehead against hers. 'This Christmas with you as my wife is a dream come true,' he whispered. 'I vow to fill all your days with joy and laughter, my darling Daphne. Our life together has only just begun.'

Daphne smiled up at him through happy tears. The future shone brightly before them, full of hope, love and the promise of many more Christmas blessings yet to come.

The grand hall was filled with warmth and merriment as Daphne and Edward returned to the rest of the guests. Sophie's eyes sparkled as she took Nigel's arm leading him over to where Daphne was pouring herself some lemonade. They stood together, faces aglow, as Nigel whispered something that made Sophie laugh gaily.

Daphne felt her heart swell at the sight. Taking Edward's hand, she gave it a loving squeeze. He smiled down at her, joy lighting his eyes.

Just then, the clock chimed the hour. Their family and friends turned expectantly as Lord Brookshire raised his glass.

'Let us toast this magical Christmas night,' he proclaimed, 'and give thanks for the bonds of love that unite us all.'

Glasses were lifted high amid cheers and applause. Daphne met Sophie's happy gaze, their smiles reflected in one another's faces.

The future, once shrouded in gloom, now shone brightly for both couples. Surrounded by those they held most dear, they celebrated the promise of hope, laughter and light that Christmas brought.

About the Author

Lisette Davenport Lives in Australia with her husband, daughter and four cats. She writes the charming Whispers series of regency romance.

You can connect with me on:

- https://lisettedavenport.wordpress.com
- https://www.facebook.com/Lisette.Davenport
- https://www.instagram.com/lisette_davenport_author

Also by Lisette Davenport

Whispers series

Whispers of the heart
After years abroad, Genevieve St. Claire returns to London's high society hoping to make a suitable match. But when she reconnects with Sebastian Mordesley, the roguishly charming Marquis of Mordesley, old passions ignite. Despite their scandalous past and Sebastian's rakish reputation, Genevieve finds herself drawn to him again.

As gossip spreads, Genevieve must choose between propriety and following her heart. Can their love overcome the forces trying to tear them apart? Sebastian too faces pressure to suppress his forbidden feelings for Genevieve. In each other, they find a connection both know they shouldn't pursue but cannot resist. Whispers of the Heart is a sweeping historical romance about duty, desire, and defying convention for love.